D0581836

A GUINEA PIG

Romeo & Juliet

A GUINEA PIG

Romeo & Juliet

A pair of star-crossed lovers...

AN ADAPTATION OF THE ORIGINAL BY

Mr. WILLIAM SHAKESPEARE

LONDON

BLOOMSBURY PUBLISHING, BEDFORD SQUARE.

2017

TROUPE OF ACTORS

MARLIN

BEAR

BILLIE

MABEL

OSCAR

SHERLOCK

MOLLY

DRAMATIS PERSONAE

ROMEO
of Montague

JULIET
of Capulet

MERCUTIO
Friend to Romeo

PRINCE OF VERONA
Keeper of the peace

TYBALT
Cousin to Juliet

FRIAR LAWRENCE
A monk

NURSE
Chaperone to Juliet

Three times have the great families of Capulet and Montague fought in the streets of Verona. To keep the peace, the Prince of Verona declares that if these mortal foes disturb the quiet again, they will pay with their lives.

Two households, both alike in dignity,
In fair Verona, where we lay our scene…

❋ ACT I ❋

Mercutio finds a lovesick Romeo walking in a grove of sycamore trees.

MERCUTIO: Good morning, Romeo.

ROMEO: Is the day so young? Ay me, sad hours seem long.

MERCUTIO: What sadness lengthens Romeo's hours?

ROMEO: In sadness, cousin, I love Rosaline,
yet she'll not be hit with Cupid's arrow.

ROMEO: *The all-seeing sun*
Never saw her match since first the world begun.

Mercutio invites Romeo to a banquet being held by the Capulets, hoping that Romeo will see other women more beautiful than Rosaline and be cured of his lovesickness.

MERCUTIO: At this same ancient feast of Capulet
Are all the admired beauties of Verona.
Compare Rosaline with some that I shall show,
And I will make thee think thy swan a crow.

Romeo and Mercutio set off for the Capulet banquet.

MERCUTIO: Come, gentle Romeo, the feast is done
And we shall come too late. We must have you dance.

ROMEO: *I fear too early, for my mind misgives*
Some consequence yet hanging in the stars...

Meanwhile in the Capulet household Juliet's Nurse gives her the surprising news that Paris, the local nobleman, wishes to marry her.

NURSE: Now you are almost fourteen, Juliet, tell me,
How stands your disposition to be married?

JULIET: It is an honour I dream not of.

NURSE: Well, think of marriage now:
The valiant Paris seeks you for his love
And does await you at the feast tonight.

Enter a servant to escort Juliet to the banquet.

NURSE: Go, girl, seek happy nights to happy days.

Romeo and Mercutio enter the banquet. Romeo forgets all about Rosaline when he sees Juliet.

ROMEO: What lady's that?
O, she doth teach the torches to burn bright...

ROMEO: *Did my heart love till now? Forswear it, sight,*
For I ne'er saw true beauty till this night.

Romeo approaches Juliet to take her hand.

ROMEO: If I profane with my unworthiest hand
This holy shrine, the gentle sin is this:
My two lips, two blushing pilgrims, ready stand
To smooth that rough touch with a tender kiss.

Juliet says it is no sin to hold hands.

JULIET: Good pilgrim, you do wrong your hand too much,
Which mannerly devotion shows in this:
For saints have hands that pilgrims' hands do touch,
And palm to palm is holy palmers' kiss.

Juliet says that lips, like hands, should be used in prayer. Romeo asks if he might 'pray' to her...

ROMEO: Have not saints lips, and holy palmers too?

JULIET: Ay, pilgrim, lips that they must use in prayer.

ROMEO: O, then, dear saint, let lips do what hands do:
                    They pray – grant thou, lest faith turn to despair.

JULIET: Saints do not move, though grant for prayers' sake.

Romeo leans forward to kiss her.

ROMEO: Then move not, while my prayer's effect I take.

The Nurse takes Juliet away, but Juliet keeps looking back at Romeo.

JULIET: What is yond gentleman, Nurse?

NURSE: His name is Romeo, and a Montague.
            The only son of your great enemy.

JULIET: *My only love sprung from my only hate!*
Too early seen unknown, and known too late!

❀ ACT II ❀

Romeo leaves the banquet when he discovers that Juliet is a Capulet, but then changes his mind.

ROMEO: Can I go forward when my heart is there?
           Turn back Romeo, and seek Juliet.

Romeo climbs over the wall and into the Capulet garden. He looks up and sees a light in a bedroom window.

ROMEO: *But soft! What light through yonder window breaks?*
It is the east, and Juliet is the sun.

Juliet laments that Romeo is a Montague, but Romeo replies that he does not care about the rift between their families. They exchange vows of love and plan to marry the next day.

JULIET: O Romeo, Romeo! Wherefore art thou Romeo?
What's in a name? That which we call a rose
By any other name would smell as sweet.

ROMEO: It is my soul that calls upon my name.
Call me but love, and I'll be new baptized.

JULIET: If that thy bent of love be honourable,
Thy purpose marriage, send me word to-morrow.

JULIET: *Goodnight, goodnight! Parting is such sweet sorrow,*
That I shall say goodnight till it be morrow.

The next morning, Romeo asks Friar Lawrence to marry him to Juliet.

ROMEO:　　　　Holy father, my heart's dear love is set
On the fair daughter of rich Capulet.
I'll tell thee more anon, but this I pray,
That thou consent to marry us today.

Friar Lawrence agrees, sensing that this marriage could heal the grudge between the Montagues and Capulets.

FRIAR: For this alliance may so happy prove
To turn your households' rancour to pure Love.

Juliet impatiently waits in her bedroom while the Nurse talks to Romeo about plans for the wedding. When the Nurse returns, Juliet pesters her for news.

JULIET: Sweet, sweet, sweet Nurse, tell me, what says my love? What says Romeo?

NURSE: Have you got leave to go to church today?

JULIET: I have.

NURSE: Then hie you hence to Friar Lawrence's church.
There stays you a husband to make you a wife.

Romeo and Friar Lawrence wait for Juliet at the church.

ROMEO: Do thou but close our hands with holy words,
Then love-devouring death do what he dare,
It is enough I may but call her mine.

Enter Juliet, running late.

FRIAR: Here comes the lady.

FRIAR: So smile the heavens upon this holy act...

❋ ACT III ❋

Juliet's hot-headed cousin Tybalt challenges Romeo to a duel because he dared to come to the Capulet banquet, but Mercutio steps forward instead.

TYBALT: Romeo, thou art a villain. Turn and draw!

MERCUTIO: Come, sir, I am for you.

Tybalt and Mercutio fight. Tybalt thrusts his sword and strikes Mercutio.

MERCUTIO: I am hurt.
            A plague on both your houses!

He dies.

ROMEO: Now, Tybalt, Mercutio's soul
Is but a little way above our heads.
Either thou or I, or both, must go with him.

Romeo vanquishes Tybalt, then flees Verona as the Prince arrives and declares Romeo's fate.

PRINCE: Who began this bloody fray?
Romeo slew Tybalt, Tybalt slew Mercutio?
Let Romeo hence in haste,
Else, when he is found, that hour is his last.

PRINCE: *I will be deaf to pleading and excuses:*
Romeo is banishèd.

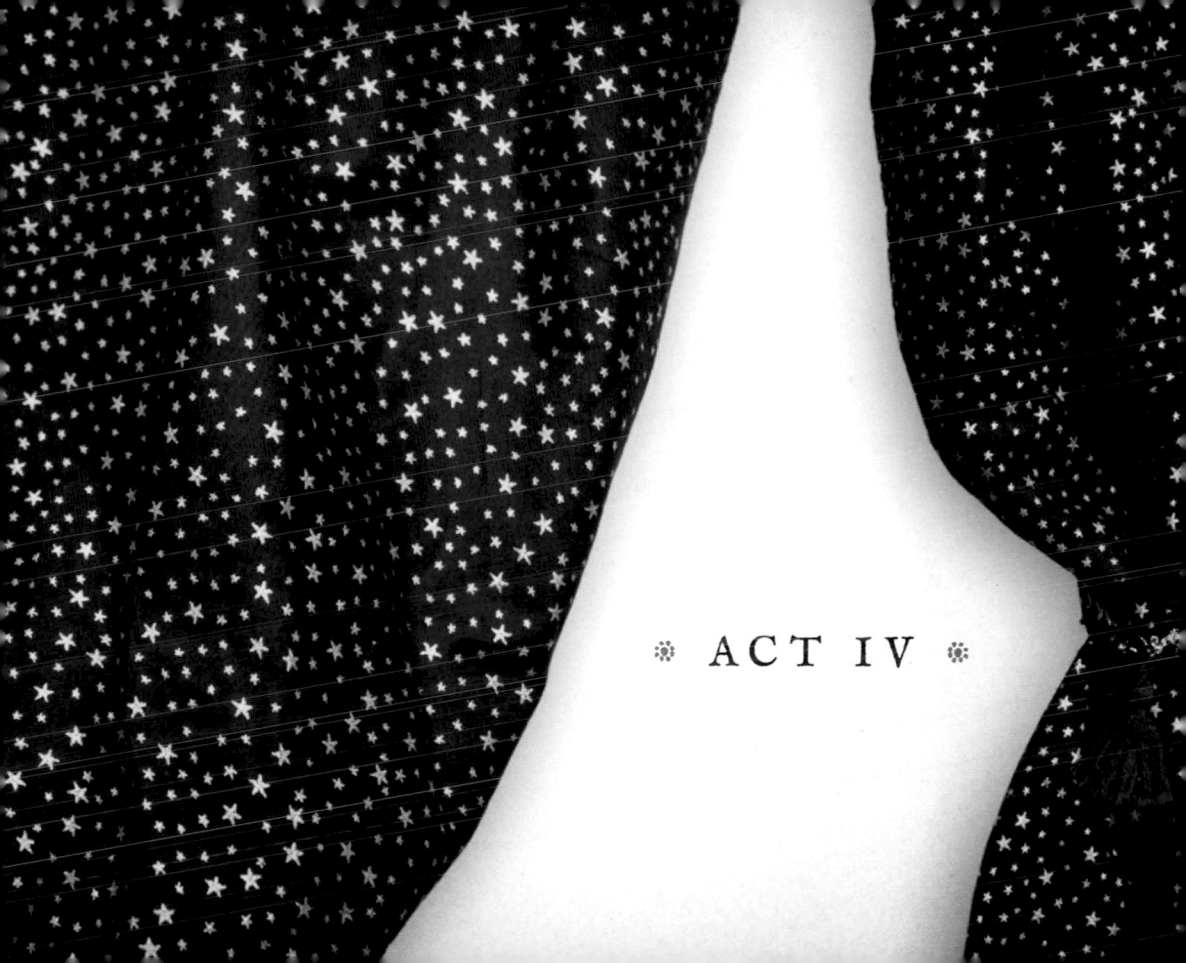

* ACT IV *

In despair at Romeo's banishment, Juliet visits Friar Lawrence to seek guidance; he gives her a sleeping potion that he says will help reunite her with Romeo.

FRIAR: Hold, daughter; I do spy a kind of hope.
Take thou this vial, being then in bed.
No warmth, no breath, shall testify thou livest;
Thou shalt be as dead two and forty hours,
And then awake as from a pleasant sleep.
That very night shall Romeo bear thee
Hence to Mantua.

JULIET: *Romeo, Romeo, Romeo! I drink to thee.*

In the morning, the Nurse comes in to wake Juliet but finds she cannot rouse her.

NURSE: Mistress! why, lady! fie, you slug-a-bed!
             Why, love, I say! madam! sweet heart!
             Marry and amen! How sound she is asleep!
             I must needs wake you. Lady, lady, lady!

NURSE: *Alas, alas! Help, help! My lady's dead!*

ACT V

Mantua. Romeo meets a messenger bearing news of the death of Juliet.

ROMEO: News from Verona! How now, messenger?
Does thou not bring me letters from the Friar?
How fares my Juliet?

MESSENGER: Her body sleeps in Capulet's tomb,
And her immortal part with angels lives.

ROMEO: Is it so? Then I defy you, stars!

ROMEO: *My Juliet, I will lie with thee tonight.
I will buy a dram of poison.*

Romeo arrives at the Capulet tomb in Verona where Juliet lies.

ROMEO: Oh my love, my wife! Eyes, look your last,
Arms, take your last embrace; and lips...

He drinks the poison.

ROMEO: *Thus with a kiss I die.*

Juliet wakes from her drugged sleep and discovers Romeo lifeless beside her. She kisses him one last time, and decides that she would rather share his fate than live without him.

JULIET: Poison, I see, hath been his timeless end.
I kiss thy lips... thy lips are warm!

JULIET: *I'll be brief. O happy dagger,*
I am thy sheath; there rest, and let me die.

The Prince arrives and summons the rival families of Romeo and Juliet to show them the price of their feud.

PRINCE: A glooming peace this morning with it brings,
            The sun, for sorrow, will not show his head.
            For never was a story of more woe
            Than this of Juliet and her Romeo.

The Montagues and Capulets pledge to live in peace and never forget their beloved Romeo and Juliet.

Come, gentle night, and turn them into stars
And they will make the face of heaven so fine
That all the world will be in love with night.

WILLIAM SHAKESPEARE was born in Stratford-upon-Avon in 1564 and is widely regarded as the greatest writer in the English language. Also known as the Bard, he wrote more than thirty plays, including *Macbeth*, *Hamlet* and *A Midsummer Night's Dream*, which have been translated into every major living language and performed countless times over the past 450 years.

TESS NEWALL was born in 1987 and when she is not stitching tiny crowns or building miniature balconies she works as a freelance set designer, specializing in fashion, window displays and decorative interiors. She lives in London.

ALEX GOODWIN was born in 1985 and owns five different editions of *The Complete Works of William Shakespeare* (which he has been told is four too many). When he is not trimming soliloquies or pruning secondary characters, he works as an editor. He lives in London.

The publishers would like to thank Pauline, Rebecca, Amanda, Sophia and *ohmyguinea*'s Becky, as well as Charles, Ella, Edie, Barbara and our other friends for their kindness and for being such good company. Thanks also to the clever carpenter, Alfred. A particular thank you to photographer and designer Phillip Beresford, without whom the torches of guinea pig Verona would burn less brightly.

Small pets are abandoned every day, but the lucky ones end up in rescue centres where they can be looked after and rehomed. You may not know it, but some of these centres are devoted entirely to guinea pigs. They work with welfare organizations to give first class advice and information, as well as finding happy new homes for the animals they look after. If you, like Romeo and Juliet, dream of a more loving world, perhaps think of supporting your local rescue centre!

Bloomsbury Publishing
An imprint of Bloomsbury Publishing Plc

50 Bedford Square   1385 Broadway
London   New York
WC1B 3DP   NY 10018
UK   USA

www.bloomsbury.com

British Library Cataloguing-in-Publication Data
A catalogue record for this book is available from the British Library.

Library of Congress Cataloguing-in-Publication data has been applied for.

ISBN UK: HB: 978-1-4088-9064-6
ISBN US: HB: 978-1-63557-000-7

2 4 6 8 10 9 7 5 3 1

Costumes and props by Tess Newall
Photography and design by Phillip Beresford
Abridgement by Alex Goodwin
Illustration on page 2 by Elizabeth Stettler

Printed and bound in China by C&C Offset Printing Co., Ltd

All papers used by Bloomsbury Publishing Plc are natural, recyclable products made from wood grown in well-managed forests. Our manufacturing processes conform to the environmental regulations of the country of origin.

Contents

Chapter 1

The Joys of Twitching

WHY DO WE WATCH BIRDS? Getting on for three million of us do in Britain, at least occasionally, every year. For some of us it means a bird table outside the kitchen window, for others a regular visit to the local bird sanctuary. For the serious twitchers amongst us, it involves journeys the length and breadth of the country – and beyond – in search of some elusive "tick" of a rare sighting.

Perhaps it's because we envy their ability to fly. Birds are all around us, everywhere, whether we live in the town or the country, on the coast or inland. We share our environment with them. And yet they live in a quite different world too, a world "up there" made pos-

sible by flight and by ancient instinctive patterns of breeding and migration, a world still regulated by the climate and the seasons from which in the modern

age we have insulated ourselves. Perhaps this is why they appear in so many tales of primitive folklore and legend – they are not bound by the same constraints as us.

If we envy their flight, we certainly admire their plumage for its infinite complexity and variety of pattern. In Britain alone it is possible to see over 400 different species of bird, amongst which even the commonest little brown bird, the House Sparrow, has graceful and subtle markings. We can be as pleased to see the Sparrow in Britain as we are the Heron or the Kestrel, the Woodpecker or the Robin – all beautiful birds.

There is beauty and pattern too in the songs of the birds. From the conversational Crow to the angelic Skylark, birdsong contains music of great variety and inspiration. The dawn chorus, the lone Mistle Thrush, even the raucous shouting of the rookery, all have the power to intrigue and lift our spirits.

Whatever your reason for watching birds – scientific, aesthetic or just plain fun – they are there for the watching, wherever you are. Enjoy them!

Chapter 2

How to Use this Book

BIRDS ARE ARRANGED IN THIS book within the relevant section. The sections reflect the general habitats in which you are most likely to see each bird, but it should be borne in mind that many birds can be seen in different habitats at different times of the year.

The book is designed as a field companion and offers accurate and useful descriptions of the 72 featured birds, and each contains further details and background information.

The book aims particularly to help the birdwatcher avoid common mistakes of wrongful identification, with notes for each bird on similar-looking species and clear references in brackets – for example Cormorant (Coastal 12) –

to the habitat section and number of the look-alike for easy comparison.

There is a further Quick Reference section at the end of the book with simple guides for sorting out three frequent sources of confusion – the Big Black Birds, the Little Brown Birds, and the Gulls.

Chapter 3

The Country Habitat

FROM CORNISH MOOR TO THE wetlands of eastern England, from the gentle South Downs to the jagged Cairngorms, there exists in Britain's countryside a remarkable diversity of natural environment. Dense forestry and scrubby heathland, open water and rocky gorge, cultivated field and fragile marsh – all offer their own solutions as breeding and feeding territories for our birdlife.

Some birds thrive in windy places; others need slow-flowing water; others still wait for the hand and plough of man to turn the soil for them. Some take their prey from remote lakes; others eat insects in ancient woodland. Each area provides a particular combi-nation of weather and shelter, sustaining an interdependent community of plant and animal life; and although individual species may occur elsewhere, every local eco-system is irreplaceably unique.

The country habitat defines the variety of our bird population just as surely as it does our human one. Like us, birds have adapted to specific resources and climate, or migrated to one which suited their needs.

Our countryside plays host to a colourful mixture of resident and migrant species, whether they are Great Crested Grebes escaping the harsh eastern European winter, or Swallows fleeing the height of an African summer, or indigenous

Curlews moving between marsh and moor within our borders.

Britain has more than 300 regularly inhabitant birds, with half as many again appearing as occasional or accidental visitors. Of this total, around 40 are in forms unique to our islands. So for example our Robin is biologically distinct from the other 7 "races" of Robin to be found in the world. And although our common Song Thrush Turdus philomelos is also common in the rest of Europe, a sub-species Turdus philomelos hebridensis is only found in the Outer Hebrides of Scotland.

Such wonderful biodiversity within our small island means that every part of the countryside has something special to offer the birdwatcher.

1. Rook

ROOKS ARE VERY GREGARIOUS birds, congregating in large groups of nests (rookeries), a familiar sight in tall trees all over Britain, where their apparent bickering with and stealing from their neighbours is accompanied by those hauntingly raucous calls.

Country lore holds that the higher the Rooks think it safe to build the nests in their treetop colonies, the better the summer is going to be. Curiously, colonies of seals are also known as rookeries, perhaps because of the

similarities in denseness of population and the harsh barking din that both creatures make!

In Ireland, if a Rook was seen to peer down a chimney, it warned of a coming death in the household. This may be connected with the old belief that every Rook had three drops of the devil's blood in it!

In fact Rooks are very likeable birds, intelligent and sociable. Although they cause some damage to young crops, they are not the threat to young livestock that for example the Carrion Crow sometimes is.

CORVUS FRUGILEGUS

Appearance: large black bird. Black all over, except for a patch of bare pale off-white skin at the base of the bill, which is quite thin and straight; slightly angled forehead. Close up, the black of the adult bird has a purple sheen to it. Thigh feathers of both adults and juveniles are long and shaggy, giving them a baggy-trousered look.

Size: 45cm (18").

Voice: drawn-out caw, as well as other shorter croaks.

Habitat: lowland farming country, in rows of trees, copses, and woodland

Distribution: all year throughout Britain and Ireland except far north of Scotland.

Not to be confused with: the Carrion Crow (Country 3), which has a shorter bill and a flatter forehead; the Raven, much bigger at 63cm (25"); and the much smaller Jackdaw (Country 5) with its grey not black hooded head.

2. Lapwing

(also called PEEWIT, GREEN PLOVER)

THE LAPWING IS BRITAIN'S commonest wader. In flight, it can be recognised by its surprisingly rounded wings, and by the lapping sound they make as they beat (hence one of its many names).

It is a familiar sight on farmland, where it gathers outside the breeding season with other birds including Golden Plovers and Black-Headed Gulls. It shares the habit of some gulls in

VANELLUS VANELLUS

Appearance: white underparts, grey back with iridescent purple and green; black sides, throat, chin and crown with distinctive long black crest rising from the back of the head; white cheeks and short thin black bill; easily missed flash of chestnut brown under the tail; pink legs. Flight reveals white under-wings and white bar at end of black tail.

Size: 30cm (12").

Voice: distinctive and plaintive pee-wit cry in flight.

Habitat: nests in damp fields and uplands. In winter, gathers in huge flocks on marsh-land, estuaries and mudflats.

Distribution: all year throughout Britain and Ireland.

Not to be confused with: the Golden Plover, which in flight also shows white underwings and in winter even has a white belly (black in summer). But the Plover has golden brown speckled upper parts, and the lapwing is really unmistakable because of its distinctive black and white plumage and crest.

drumming the ground with its feet. This is in imitation of raindrops landing, and has the effect of bringing insects up to the surface where they think they will escape drowning.

Faced with predators, the Lapwing flies away and then makes a lot of noise when farthest from the nest, to draw intruders towards her and away from her vulnerable young – a false-alarm tactic which Shakespeare used as a metaphor for insincerity:

"Far from her nest the lapwing cries away" (Comedy of Errors).

3. **Woodpigeon**

(also called RING DOVE)

THE WOODPIGEON'S ALTERNATIVE name, Ring Dove, could be confused with that of the Collared Dove, which is however quite different in appearance.

It used to be believed that pigeons always hatched two eggs, one male and one female, and that these two would live together in love for the rest of their lives. Because of this, boy and girl human twins were sometimes called a pigeon pair.

In Ireland the pigeon was one of many birds associated with death; it was believed to accompany funeral processions, and therefore a pigeon visiting a farmyard which did not already hold pigeons was considered unlucky.

Plump pigeons and doves have been a plentiful and easy supply of meat since

COLUMBA PALUMBUS

Appearance: plump grey dove with relatively small head; yellow and black eye; pink-tinged chest, white patch either side of neck; small reddish-pink bill and legs. White wing-bars before dark tail and wingtips are revealed in flight.

Size: 40cm (16").

Voice: a soothing five-note phrase – cu-COO-coo, coo-coo.

Habitat: all kinds of wooded area; feeds in open spaces.

Distribution: all year, throughout Britain and Ireland.

Not to be confused with: smaller members of the dove family such as the Rock Dove (rare, confined to wilder Scottish and Irish coasts, no white marks, bold black wing-bars, grey wing-tips), the Stock Dove (widespread except in parts of Ireland and the Scottish Highlands, no white marks, shorter tail, black wing-tips), and the Feral Pigeon (Urban 13) (thinner and scruffier!).

at least the Bronze Age. Man has often encouraged them to roost in or near human habitation, through the provision of dove-cotes, and there are written references to them as long ago as 685 AD in the works of the scholastic Saint Aldhelm of Malmesbury.

Despite its cheerful, puffed-up, almost Dickensian appearance, the Woodpigeon is a major countryside pest, doing an enormous amount of damage by feeding on young crops.

4. Carrion Crow

THE HOODED CROW (CORVUS corone cornix) is a close cousin of the Carrion Crow, found where the Carrion Crow is not – Ireland, the Isle of Man and the Scottish Highlands. It differs in appearance by having a distinct mid-grey rather than black body beneath its black wings and black head.

Unlike the Rook which it so closely resembles, the Carrion or Hooded Crow is a solitary bird, nesting and feeding alone or in close family groups – very occasionally foraging in small gangs, or flocks of a few hundred.

The "Hoodie" is said to have a deeper voice than the Carrion Crow. The familiar sound of either crow at dusk was a

useful bedtime reminder for children in the days before clocks and TV. An old rhyme goes:

> "*Caw, caw!*" *says the crow, as he flies overhead,*
> "*It's time little Mary [or Johnny] was going to bed.*"

Easy to characterise as unpleasant because they are black and scavenge for dead meat, the collective noun for these birds is a murder of crows! But the crow is actually one of Britain's most intelligent animals, adapting ingeniously to the man-made environment. It can be seen in parks taking stale bread to the pond to soften it for example, and has learnt to haul up bin liners like fishing nets from deep bins to get at the discarded food at the bottom of them.

CORVUS CORONE CORONE

Appearance: large black bird. All black, with a faint green gloss on the back; featherless black legs, heavy black beak and face; in flight, square-cut tail and relatively blunt, rounded wingtips.

Size: 47cm (19").

Voice: short harsh kaa-kaa-kaa.

Habitat: open countryside with a few trees – not denser woodland.

Distribution: all year throughout England, Wales and southern Scotland.

Not to be confused with: the Rook (Country 1), which has a higher forehead, a whitish face and a purple sheen on its back; the Raven, a much bigger black bird with a different habitat; and the Jackdaw (Country 5), which has dark grey underparts, paler grey neck and back of head, a shorter bill and a black cap and forehead.

5. Jackdaw

THE JACKDAW IS ANOTHER sociable member of the crow family, not quite as communal as the Rook but often found in that bird's company and in large groups of other Jackdaws. It is a nimble bird, both on foot and in the air where it occasionally offers aerobatic displays.

It is relatively unafraid of humans, and can be easily tamed (although it can be quite a bully on the bird table in hard winters). There are many historical examples of the Jackdaw being kept as a pet.

The Jackdaw is much mentioned in folklore. One Jackdaw perched on a

CORVUS MONEDULA

Appearance: large blackish bird. Black wings and back, dark grey underbody, with a hood which varies from dark grey to off-white; distinctive pale grey eyes; a high black forehead and a relatively short bill.

Size: 29cm (12").

Voice: high-pitched chuck-chuck.

Habitat: open woodland and well-wooded parkland; also nests in old buildings and sheltered inland cliffs.

Distribution: all year throughout Britain and Ireland, but less common in north west Scotland.

Not to be confused with: the slightly larger and all-black Rook (Country 1), with which it frequently associates (often even nesting in abandoned rooks' nests); the Chough is similar in flight but is all-black with a distinctive slender curved deep orange bill and orange legs, and is much rarer with only a few nesting sites on western coasts of Ireland and Britain.

rooftop was a sign of bad luck, but several were an omen of good financial fortune. Aesop has several fables about the bird – The Jackdaw and the String, The Jackdaw and the Doves, The Vain Jackdaw, The Eagle and the Jackdaw, The Jackdaw and the Fox – all concerned with the bird's wily nature.

Like the Magpie, the Jackdaw has a reputation for mischievous thieving, as featured in an early 19th century short story called The Jackdaw of Rheims in which a Jackdaw steals a cardinal's ring. (The cardinal curses the unknown thief, the curse makes the Jackdaw dishevelled and the bird's guilt is revealed!)

6. Magpie

WITH ITS CLEAN LINES AND subtly rich colouring, the Magpie is one

of Britain's beautiful birds. But it is also an extremely aggressive coloniser, attacking and eating small and young birds and eggs when it moves into an area, extremely annoying to gamekeepers. Farmers dislike it because it feeds on grain. But it also eats vermin, insects and other farmland pests.

Usually seen in groups of two or three, the Magpie can assemble in larger numbers at times of display or roosting. This observation gave rise to the traditional rhymes about magpie numbers, one of which goes:

One's sorrow, two's mirth,
Three's a wedding, four's a birth,
Five's a christening, six a death,
Seven's heaven, eight is hell,
And nine's the devil his ane sel'.

More familiar to viewers of the 70s and 80s children's TV series Magpie will be the version used in the programme's theme tune:

One for sorrow, two for joy,
Three for a girl and four for a boy,
Five for silver, six for gold,
Seven for a secret never to be told.

The magazine series was so named because of the Magpie's attraction to all sorts of shiny objects, which it collects and hordes in its nest.

In folklore it has associations with witchcraft and bad luck. In some parts of the country, a Magpie spotted on its own must be formally greeted – "Good morning, Mr Magpie!" – to avert bad luck. In Devon, seeing a Magpie brought ill fortune which could only be prevented by spitting three times. In Scotland a death was forewarned by Magpies flying near to a household's windows.

The name, a corruption of the older version maggot-pie, may derive from marguerite (the Old French word for a white pearl) and pied (meaning black and white). The old country name for both the bird and the pretty white marguerite daisy was Margaret.

PICA PICA

Appearance: distinctive black and white bird. Black head, body and wings, with sharply defined white belly and a long black tail, the tail and wings tinged with iridescent greens, blues and purples when seen at close quarters.

Size: 45cm (18").

Voice: harsh rattling chatter in short or longer bursts; warning chack-chack.

Habitat: open farming country, open woodland.

Distribution: all year throughout Ireland and Britain except the far north of Scotland.

Not to be confused with: anything else! The Magpie is unmistakable.

7. Great Spotted Woodpecker

(also called PIED WOODPECKER)

USUALLY HEARD BEFORE IT IS seen, the woodpecker gets its name from its habit of hammering resonantly on dry wood. This announces its presence to other woodpeckers of course, but may also have the effect of stirring up the larvae of wood-boring insects, on which it feeds.

The alternative names of the Great and Lesser Spotted Woodpecker also help to distinguish them: the Great is also known as the Pied Woodpecker because its plumage appears at a glance to be large solid patches of black and white; the Lesser,

sometimes called the Barred Woodpecker, has those distinctive white bars across its back.

DENDROCOPUS MAJOR

Appearance: black back and white breast, black wings with a white flash and narrow white bars at the ends, bright splash of red feathers under the longish tail; beige-white forehead and white around the eyes, black cap (red in juveniles) and a band of red on the back of the neck, with bands of black running from it to the bill and wings. The female adult lacks the red on the neck.

Size: 23cm (9").

Voice: a short sharp chick, usually single but sometimes repeated to form a chattering sound.

Habitat: woodland both conifer and deciduous, and well-wooded open ground including orchards and gardens.

Distribution: throughout Britain except the very far north, absent from Ireland.

Not to be confused with: the Lesser Spotted Woodpecker (Dendrocopus minor), which is much smaller at 15cm (6"); the Lesser male retains in adulthood the red cap that both it and the Great Spotted Woodpecker had as juveniles. The Lesser also has clear white bars on its back, wings and tail feathers, and lacks the Great's flash of red under the tail. The Lesser Spotted Woodpecker has a different call (a high-pitched pee-pee-pee) and is also much rarer, confined largely to England and Wales.

8. Kestrel

IN HIGH WINDS THE KESTREL CAN remain motionless in the sky with tiny adjustments of tail and wing feathers; in still air it remains equally still except for the rapid beating of its wings. From a hovering height of 15m (50ft) it will drop like a stone on its prey of small rodents and large insects.

Britain's birds of prey are experiencing something of a revival, having gone into serious decline for much of the

20th century at the hands of hunters, egg collectors and aggressive farming techniques. The Osprey for example has reappeared in a few locations and both the Peregrine and the Sparrowhawk, though still scarce, have recovered from near-extinction.

FALCO TINNUNCULUS

Appearance: reddish brown back, speckled black in the male, barred black in the female; black tail- and wing-tips; yellowish brown speckled breast; short hooked yellow bill and bright yellow legs; head and tail grey in the male, reddish brown in the female and juvenile, black moustache-like lines below bright yellow eyes.

Size: 35cm (14").

Voice: high-pitched kee-kee-kee, often while flying; in alarm, more of a keh-keh-keh.

Habitat: open fields, open woodland, moorland, rocky coastal areas.

Distribution: all year throughout Ireland and Britain except Shetland.

Not to be confused with: the Sparrowhawk, which has slate-grey upper parts and russet and buff (male) or pale grey and black (female) close-barred underparts; and the Merlin, slightly smaller with a blue-grey (male) or muddy brown (female) back; the Peregrine is slightly larger, with blue-grey upper parts and off-white underparts with narrow grey-brown barring.

However, although the Kestrel is the most familiar and numerous of our birds of prey, it remains in decline. It has successfully adapted to environments in town, country and coastline precisely because farming methods are eradicating its prey from its traditional farmland hunting grounds. This is why we see and admire it so often at the roadside – it has been forced to hunt there.

9. **Meadow Pipit**

LIKE ALL PIPITS, THE MEADOW Pipit has a diet of insects, mostly taken as it ambles about (walking, not hopping) on the ground. All Pipits nest at ground level, making a little grassy cup on the ground amidst longer grassland, where they lay one or two clutches of four or five eggs a year. (Only the Red-Throated Pipit of eastern Europe never produces a second brood, something which is only possible in the longer breeding season allowed by our more temperate western climates.)

The Pipits are a family of rich variety in many aspects, but unfortunately not

ANTHUS PRATENSIS

Appearance: speckled brown bird. Greeny brown upper parts, off-white underparts with long dark brown streaks; unusually long hind-claws; dark pink-brown legs, lighter pink in juveniles.

Size: 14cm (5").

Voice: gets its name from the shrill seep-seep-seep, called from ground, low shrub or ascending flight; descending flight accompanied by a song of accelerating tinkling notes ending in a trill.

Habitat: any open ground where there is grass, from heathland to sand-dune.

Distribution: all year throughout Britain and Ireland, commoner in the north and west.

Not to be confused with: the Woodlark (which has a shorter tail); the Skylark (Country 10) (slightly larger, has a crest); the Tree Pipit (yellower brown upper parts, paler legs, calls from trees); and the Rock Pipit (Coastal 24) (coastal habitat, greyer, slightly larger).

in their appearance! With minor variations they are all basically like so many little brown birds, impossible at a glance to tell apart. Understandably it was only relatively recently, in the 18th century, that ornithologists learnt to differentiate between the various British Pipit species.

The migratory schedules of Pipits and the habitats reflected in their names are the key distinctions. In places and at times when two may overlap, the song is the identifying feature. The Tree Pipit for example has a harsher "treese" call than the Meadow Pipit, and ends its descending flight song with a very distinctive "see-ya see-ya see-ya". The Rock Pipit has a similar call and song to the Meadow Pipit's, but a fuller more rounded voice.

10. Skylark

ANOTHER LITTLE BROWN BRITISH bird, unremarkable in appearance, reveals itself as a national treasure when it starts to sing. The unrestrained stream of joyful notes can be heard at almost any time of year, but particularly from late winter to midsummer, when a bright sunny dawn will be enough to send the Skylark, and our spirits, soaring.

The bird sings from the moment it leaves the ground, rising to become little more than a speck in the sky, and continues to sing as it descends, stopping only to fold its wings back in the final stages and drop once more to the ground.

The song of the Skylark is a frequent subject of poetry, for example in this typical eulogy by the 16th century poet John Lyly:

> *None but the lark so shrill and clear;*
> *How at heaven's gates she claps her wings,*
> *The morn not waking till she sings.*

The Skylark has also inspired musical composers, most famously Vaughan Williams whose haunting piece The Lark Ascending is one of the finest man-made evocations of bird-song ever written.

ALAUDA ARVENSIS

Appearance: speckled brown bird. Earthy brown striped back; off-white belly and speckled brown breast; inconspicuous crest; pale cheeks and dark ring around eye interrupted by white eyebrow; long hind-claws like the meadow pipit. Juveniles have a shorter tail like the woodlark.

Size: 18cm (7").

Voice: continuous bubbly chirping for extended periods (from just a few minutes to as many as 15), usually in flight.

Habitat: all sorts of open wild or farmed countryside.

Distribution: all year throughout Britain and Ireland; less common in north west Scotland.

Not to be confused with: the Crested Lark, which has a more obvious triangular crest; the Woodlark with its smaller, shorter tail; and the Meadow Pipit (Country 9), a smaller bird with a different, more metallic, song.

11. Stonechat

UNFORTUNATELY THE STONECHAT population has been declining in recent years. Dependent on a diet of insects, spiders and worms, it is particularly vulnerable to two separate threats – intensive farming methods, and harsh winter seasons – both of which can remove its food sources and severely affect numbers.

Although local populations can recover from the occasional fierce

SAXICOLA TORQUATA

Appearance: male has black-brown back, head and eye; white patch on side of neck; a beige belly with a rust-red breast; thin black legs. Flight reveals pale rump and white bar on wing, pale rump. Female and juvenile have mottled brown and black head and back; juvenile has mottled brown and beige belly and chest.

Size: 12cm (4").

Voice: rasping whit-chat-chat from high perches, and short bursts of a whistling high-pitched warble in flight.

Habitat: heathland, both inland and above coastal cliffs.

Distribution: all year throughout Britain and Ireland, especially on coasts; rarer in eastern England.

Not to be confused with: the Whinchat, a summer-only visitor, which is slightly larger and slimmer; both male and female Whinchats have a whitish eyebrow and browner back and head; and the Robin (Urban 8), another redbreast of course but of much bolder orange-red which extends to the face; and the Robin's upper parts are brown, not black.

winter, the use of pesticides and the destruction of its wild country habitat by farmers and builders are more persistent threats to the bird. The Stonechat is increasingly confined to softer coastal regions, which are milder and relatively safe from development and reclamation.

The Stonechat typically perches on a bush of gorse to watch for its prey, dropping down to seize it before return-ing to its perch to eat. The poet William Wordsworth, a keen observer of nature, described this animated behaviour in his poem "Addressed To A Young Lady":

> *…By lichens grey, and scant moss o'ergrown;*
> *Where scarce the foxglove peeps, or thistle's beard;*
> *And restless stone-chat all day long is heard.*

12. Swallow

PROBABLY THE MOST FAMILIAR migrant visitor to Britain, flocks of Swallows arriving in the spring are a welcome sight – the saying that one Swallow doesn't make a summer has arisen precisely because their arrival means summer is just around the corner.

The Swallow is one of the most agile of flyers. It darts back and forth making spectacular changes of direction with impossibly sharp turns in the search for airborne insects at the end of the day. It flies lower and generally takes larger prey than the House Martin.

HIRUNDO RUSTICA

Appearance: dark steel-blue back, head and throat; reddish chin and forehead; short slim bill; white under parts; long forked tail (longer on male than female).

Size: 19cm (8").

Voice: a twittering swit-swit; song from perch or in flight a series of clicks, squeaks and distinctive trills.

Habitat: nests on beams and ledges in out-buildings near rich farm and grasslands.

Distribution: April to October throughout Britain and Ireland.

Not to be confused with: the Swift, which has no white markings and a shorter forked tail; and the House Martin (Urban 11) with its much shorter fork, white rump and no red markings.

As a rule, Swallows nest inside buildings, House Martins under the eaves outside – the Swallow's nest is an open bowl, while the House Martin's is more enclosed, with an entrance above. And while Swallows and House Martins both form those familiar lines perched on overhead cables, Swifts never do.

A Scandinavian legend says that the bird gets its name from having hovered over Christ on the cross, repeatedly squeaking "svala!" ("be comforted!"). Perhaps this is why it is still considered good luck to have a Swallow nesting on your property, especially if it flies into the house. Conversely, one old country belief held that if a farmer tried to get rid of Swallows or their nests, his cows would start to milk blood.

13. **Heron**

IN FLIGHT THE GREY HERON can seem ungainly, almost prehistoric, with its slow heavy wing strokes – neck hunched up, legs trailing behind like ribbons. But it is also stately, unhurried, majestic, unique among British birds.

On land it's an opportunistic hunter which can be found at almost any type of water feature, man-made or natural – coastal saltmarshes, riverbanks, reed-banks, canals, even garden ponds (as many a frustrated water wildlife gardener will confirm!).

Like all birds relying on a water

ARDEA CINEREA

Appearance: tall, grey body, with a long white neck and head; bright yellow eye; black cap with long black plume running back from it; long sharp bill, pink, yellow or orange, dull except during February mating when it becomes bright; long brown legs; juvenile has grey head and neck, the neck spotted black.

Size: 94cm (37").

Voice: harsh cra-a-ack and other screeches.

Habitat: shallow water, both salt and fresh; nests in colonies called heronries in trees.

Distribution: all year throughout Ireland and Britain except Shetland.

Not to be confused with: the Purple Heron (extremely rare visitor to Britain, smaller bird with brown-grey back and body, orange-red neck and longer bill).

environment, the Heron is vulnerable to icy winters. This may explain why it is increasingly seen in urban parks, where open water is less likely to freeze in the warmer city air.

A model of patience, it typically stands motionless in the shallows with neck folded back ready to dart on its prey. But it is also known to stalk, wading cautiously through the water until it disturbs its prey, before stabbing it repeatedly with its dagger-like bill. Its diet consists not only of fish but also of frogs, rodents and even small birds.

In traditional Irish healing lore, Heron oil was supposed to be a good treatment for burns. Unfortunately it was extracted by leaving the body of a dead Heron to decompose in a manure heap for a month!

14. **Snipe**

BECAUSE THE SNIPE FEEDS BY trawling its long bill through soft mud, its habitat has been seriously curtailed by the drainage of land for leisure or building use. Dry land is of no use to the Snipe.

Similarly, frozen ground will not yield to the Snipe bill, so in the winter months the bird tends to drift to flowing fresh water and coastal marshes less prone to ice.

The Snipe is extremely well camouflaged for its marsh undergrowth habitat, and you are quite likely to be almost on top of it before you flush it out; it will then fly away with a characteristic zig-zag evasive flight. This is another key to differentiating it from its cousin the Jack Snipe – the latter flies off only a short distance, and in a low straight line.

The Snipe has been much hunted in the past for food – those who shot it were snipers, the term subsequently applied to concealed marksmen of all kinds. The snipe hunt also became a metaphor for the practical joke, following the custom of inexperienced huntsmen being sent to shoot Snipe in woodland by someone who knew full well that Snipe were actually birds of marsh and heath.

GALLINAGO GALLINAGO

Appearance: dark brown upper parts with creamy stripes; head and throat paler brown with clear dark stripes; exceptionally long bill (up to 2 times the length of the head); pale brown breast mottled with dark brown; white belly.

Size: 27cm (11").

Voice: a staccato scrip scrip when startled; in spring a repetitive musical chip-a chip-a from a perch; during breeding a drumming of air in the tail during sharply descending flight.

Habitat: muddy marshes and boggy heaths.

Distribution: all year throughout Britain and Ireland, although less common in the south.

Not to be confused with: the Jack Snipe (a smaller bird with a relatively shorter bill, and a darker brown back which shows off the cream streaks better); the Woodcock has similar markings but is larger, with a shorter bill and a woodland habitat.

15. **Tufted Duck**

THE TUFTED DUCK IS ONE OF two common British ducks (the Pochard is the other) which dives below the surface for its food (rather than dabbling for it with its rump still above water like many other species of water fowl). So it is better suited to deeper, stiller waters than for example the equally common Mallard.

The Tufted Duck builds its nest with down feathers, lining a hollow in the ground near the water's edge but concealed by long grass or reeds. It is a sociable bird, congregating in large flocks on open water, often in the company of Pochard and other ducks. Such congregations are a useful opportunity to compare and identify different species.

The Tufted Duck is almost tame in its attitude to human presence, unruffled by our approach and even coming to public parks sometimes for food. In the wild they are more likely to swim off a short distance than fly away altogether.

AYTHYA FULIGULA

Appearance: male all black except for sharply defined white flanks and belly; female dark brown with mid-brown flanks less well defined. Both have blue-grey bill, bright yellow eye and a downward-sloping crest, longer in the male; female sometimes has indistinct white around bill. Both have a white wing bar visible in flight.

Size: 43cm (17").

Voice: male a soft wheezing whistle during courtship; female a rough grumbling cur-cur.

Habitat: lakes and reservoirs.

Distribution: all year in Britain and Ireland – in winter less likely in the north and more abundant near the coast.

Not to be confused with: the Scaup, which is larger, with a heavier build – the male Scaup has a grey back and a green gloss to its black head, the female a clear white ring at base of bill; the female Pochard (Country 23) is paler brown than the female Tufted Duck, with white patch on bill.

16. Chiffchaff

THE CHIFFCHAFF IS RESIDENT in southern Europe and southern Britain, and is migrant in the rest of the country. But it arrives there so early (mid to late March) and stays later than many other visitors, so it could be mistaken for a resident throughout Britain.

Its early arrival makes the Chiffchaff's song one of the first signs of each returning spring. At the other end of the year it can be heard after most autumn migrants have already departed. The Chiffchaff builds a domed nest woven from blades of grass, either on the ground or very low in a bush above it. It feeds on tree-dwelling insects, which it will pluck from the leaves or sometimes in flight.

PHYLLOSCOPUS COLLYBITA

Appearance: buff underparts, olive-brown upper parts; round head, pale yellowish face and throat with olive-brown stripe along eye and pale stripe above it (more marked in juveniles); blackish legs.

Size: 10cm (4").

Voice: sing-song repetitive chiff-chaff from tall trees; alarm call is a rising, single wh-eet.

Habitat: woodlands and wooded gardens.

Distribution: all year throughout Britain and Ireland, but much rarer outside the south especially in winter.

Not to be confused with: the Wood Warbler, which is slightly larger, with yellower upper parts and white belly; and the Willow Warbler, a very similar, but slightly paler and yellower bird, with a greyer underside, flatter head and more pronounced eyebrow, and pale brown legs.

The great 18th century naturalist Gilbert White was the first to separately identify the Wood and Willow Warblers and the Chiffchaff, and he did so principally through their songs. So similar is the Chiffchaff to the Willow Warbler in particular that bird-watchers lacking time to distinguish between them often log them both as willow-chiffs!

There are tiny differences in addition to the songs and subtle variations in marking – for example the Willow Warbler's alarm call is more of a whoo-eet, and the Chiffchaff has a characteristic bob-down tail movement.

17. **Shoveler**

THIS IS THE WATERFOWL THAT IN the 16th century was known as the Spoonbilled Duck, and the broad flat bill, wider and rounder at the tip, is its defining characteristic. The Shoveler feeds as it swims along, with its spoon-shaped bill sweeping from side to side through the water. Thus it gathers and filters invertebrates and aquatic seeds with the help of the fine hairs which line the bill.

To reach food lying deeper in the water it will upend itself, revealing the tops of its bright orange legs with its rump and long wingtip feathers pointing to the sky. But it is primarily a sifter, not a dabbler.

The Shoveler has been known to feed in water directly above deeper diving ducks, presumably benefiting from food-bearing mud and debris disturbed by the lower birds and floating to the surface.

ANAS CLYPEATA

Appearance: male has dark green head with yellow eyes; black back, white chest and chestnut sides, with a white bar before a black tail (all colouring less pronounced in summer); pale blue forewings visible in flight. Female is a mottled pale brown all over with grey-blue forewings; both have distinctive long, broad beaks.

Size: 49cm (19").

Voice: the male makes a nasal panh, and a falling musical couplet of chuk-chuk; the female has a loud low-pitched quack.

Habitat: shallow waters with plenty of vegetation, such as reed beds or overgrown streams.

Distribution: all year throughout lowland Britain and Ireland, but rarer in the west and north, especially during breeding.

Not to be confused with: the female Mallard (Urban 20) which has a darker brown back and smaller bill than the female Shoveler, and that distinctive petrol blue on the hindwing; the male Mallard has the green head of the male Shoveler, but a brown not white breast and a yellow not black bill.

18. **Dartford Warbler**

THE DARTFORD WARBLER IS A rare and elusive bird, darting quickly from one clump of gorse to another except in the warmest weather. It is best seen during its pre-breeding display in late spring, when it performs an almost coquettish aerial dance flitting back and forth with rapid

SYLVIA UNDATA

Appearance: upper parts grey brown becoming greyer over a rounded head; startling red eye, short spiky yellow bill; russet-brown throat, chest and underparts (the throat speckled white); thin orange-yellow legs; long thin dark-grey tail.

Size: 13cm (5").

Voice: call a sharp churr; song a fast melodic chatter of low and high notes.

Habitat: gorse-covered heath and scrubland.

Distribution: southern England, chiefly Dorset and the New Forest.

Not to be confused with: the Subalpine Warbler which is very similar size and markings, but with a white moustache below the eyes – and which only occurs around the Mediterranean!

wingbeats and flicks of its tail.

The British population of the Dartford Warbler has always been at the limit of its range amongst the heather and gorse lands of southernmost England. It prefers a much warmer, drier environment, and occurs much more widely in western France, Spain and Italy. It is extremely vulnerable to our periodically harsh northern winters, which can drastically reduce its numbers, almost to the point of local extinction. For example in the fierce cold season of 1962-63 only a few pairs survived at all. Even now there are fewer than 2000 territorial pairs.

Until late last century the Dartford Warbler was Britain's only resident, as opposed to visiting, warbler. In the 1970s Cetti's Warbler began to colonise the south of England from continental Europe. Although they share a habitat, the two are very different in call and appearance, the Cetti being brown above and off-white below, with an off-white eyebrow and a generally flatter head.

19. **Wheatear**

THE 16TH CENTURY POET John Taylor wrote:

> Th'are called wheat-ears, less
> than lark or sparrow,
> Well-roasted, in the mouth
> they taste like marrow.
> ... The name of wheat-ears, on
> them is ycleped [fixed]
> Because they come when
> wheat is yearly reaped.

Taylor shows an early understanding that the Wheatear was a visitor rather than a resident, although his enjoyment of birds seems to have been different from that of the ornithologist!

In fact the Wheatear gets it name neither from ears nor wheat, but from an Old English description of it – wheat is the root of the modern English "white", and ear is the ancestor of "arse"! The same meaning is conveyed in Culblanc, the French name for the bird.

It is a ground-dwelling bird for the most part, preferring rocks and boulders to bushes and trees. It can often be seen shadowing people from in front, just bobbing a short distance on to the next outcrop, as if to keep a close eye on their progress.

A hugely successful migrant, the Wheatear travels from its African base not only to all of Britain and Europe but throughout North America to Alaska, north western Canada and Greenland.

OENANTHE OENANTHE

Appearance: male has black wings, grey back and headcap; white face with black patch across cheek and eye; buff-white underparts merging with a pale orange-red throat. Female has brown wings with pale brown back and cap, and less pronounced black eye marking; both have distinctive white tail with a bold inverted black T at the tip visible in flight.

Size: 14cm (5").

Voice: Call is a harsh chack and piercing seet; song is a warbling mixture of rough and more musical sounds.

Habitat: high grassland with scree, boulders or cliffs.

Distribution: March to October throughout Britain and Ireland, but less common in eastern England.

Not to be confused with: the Whinchat, which is slightly smaller and with a back of mottled black (male) or brown (female).

20. **Linnet**

THE LINNET MOVES AROUND IN close-knit flocks and can often be found in large numbers on open waste ground feeding on the seeds of weeds. Its names, both Latin and English, derive from its seed-eating habits: carduelis means thistle, cannabina

CARDUELIS CANNABINA

Appearance: male has orange-brown back and underparts; pale red chest; light grey head with dash of pale red on forehead (deeper red in spring) and short triangular grey bill. Female has streaked brown body, off-white under parts and speckled brown chest; brown head with a pale patch on cheeks. Both have black tail and wingtips, all with white streaks.

Size: 13cm (5").

Voice: a short, quiet, melodious warble, sometimes with a whistling chew-ee.

Habitat: uncultivated ground with hedges or bushes for food and nesting.

Distribution: all year throughout Britain and Ireland except north western Scotland.

Not to be confused with: the Redpoll (very similar but with brown back and head, and buff-white underparts); and the Twite (similar in flight but generally browner and lacking red markings).

refers to its fondness for hempseed, and Linnet reflects its taste for the seed of the flax plant, linum, from which linen is made. In Scotland it used to be called the Lintwhite, in north east England the Whin-lintie or the Lennart.

Linnets nest in small colonies, sometimes in single pairs, but are essentially very sociable birds. Rarely however will they come into gardens.

Because of its musical song, the Linnet was often kept as a caged bird, for the pleasure of invalids or others who could not see them in the wild. Following the shipwreck of the liner "Celtic" off the coast of Ireland in 1928, one man saved the caged Linnet which had belonged to the ship's purser and exhibited it in the area as The Most Widely Travelled Bird In The World!

21. **Great Crested Grebe**

THE GREAT CRESTED GREBE IS distinctive in flight with its legs trailing stiffly behind and its neck held stretched forward and slightly lowered (unlike the heron, which holds its neck awkwardly folded while flying).

The elaborate ruff and plume which appear after winter are of course an aid to this Grebe's courtship ritual, which is amongst the more spectacular of British birds. It includes many phases, including the much-filmed dance they conduct while facing each other on the water, rising up or swinging their necks from side to side. They also dive together, returning to the surface with gifts of weeds which they exchange.

Successful couples then nest on a rough raft of weeds either resting on the shallow bottom of the water or actually floating and anchored to underwater weeds, raising a brood of between three and six eggs a year.

The Great Crested Grebe was culled in great numbers in the 19th century for its spectacular plumage, which was used as an alternative to fur in ladies' clothing. Its near-extinction was the initial impetus for setting up the Royal Society for the Protection of Birds, the RSPB, in 1889.

PODICEPS CRISTATUS

Appearance: dark brown upper parts, and back of long neck; front of neck and underparts creamy white; head white with unique black tufted crest and chestnut brown ruff (crest and ruff absent in winter); black line from eye to long sharp pink bill; black legs.

Size: 48cm (19").

Voice: variety of barks, quacks, clicks and growls including a heron-like harsh cra-a-ack.

Habitat: open freshwater reservoirs, lakes and canals where aquatic vegetation is present.

Distribution: all year throughout Britain and Ireland except the north west of both countries; less common in west Wales.

Not to be confused with: the Red-Necked Grebe, a very rare visitor to eastern England in winter only, with a shorter russet-brown neck (grey-brown in winter) and yellow bill.

22. **Teal**

THE TEAL IS THE SMALLEST OF the common British ducks, noted for its agile darting flight. It is a nervous bird, sometimes flying low over a stretch of water several times before finally landing on it. It is neither a dabbling nor a diving duck, preferring to search the mud at the water's edge for plants and seeds.

The Teal has of course given its name to the brilliant blue-green colour of its hindwing. Its sharply defined markings are readily identifiable, making it the frequent subject of exaggerated ornamental reproductions.

You may occasionally be lucky enough to see the Teal's North American cousin, the Green-Winged Teal, a few of which now regularly visit Britain. An almost identical sub-species, the Green-Winged Teal differs only in the male at rest showing a vertical white stripe on its side instead of the horizontal one of the British bird.

ANAS CRECCA

Appearance: male has distinctive rounded chocolate brown head with green band (edged in very fine white line) running back from eye; dark grey bill; back and flanks mid-grey (made of very fine black and white lines); speckled brown chest, paler belly; pale yellow patch under tail edged in black. Female is almost featureless speckled brown duck in water. Both have grey wings with white central bar and bright green hindwing; in autumn male's colours are muted and closer to the female's.

Size: 35cm (14").

Voice: ringing crick-crick (male) and high-pitched quack (female).

Habitat: wet moorland and freshwater marshes; in winter on more open water.

Distribution: all year throughout Britain and Ireland.

Not to be confused with: the Garganey, whose females are very similar to female Teal, but the Garganey is a slightly larger duck with less rounded head and bold white stripe over the eye); and the Wigeon which has a fuller body, paler markings, and no green colouring).

23. Pochard

THE POCHARD'S NAME (pronounced poach-ard) may arise from its red face and eyes – pochard is a French word for a drunkard! Resident in Britain all year, its numbers are significantly increased in the autumn by migrants from Russia.

The Pochard and the Tufted Duck are Britain's two common diving ducks – they more usually swim underwater in search of food instead of dabbling – that is, remaining on the surface and "ducking" down with their heads below and their tails in the air.

Pochards can dive to depths of around a metre, and for periods of up to 60 seconds, in search of roots, shoots and seeds – unlike the Tufted Duck with whom it often associates, the Pochard is often nocturnal in its habits.

Pochards are known from fossil beds in Norfolk to have lived and died in the Britain of 500,000 years ago, when mastodons, mammoths, sabre tooth tigers, the giant beaver and the forest rhinoceros were also among the native species! So too were Cormorants, Crows and at least two other species of duck including the Shoveler.

AYTHYA FERINA

Appearance: male has pale grey body of teal-like fine black and white striped feathers, framed by black tail and chest; red-brown head with red eye. Female has mottled grey and brown body with dark tail and mid-brown chest and head; brown eye set in a fine white ring. Both have dark flattish bill with pale grey patch; male generally drabber in summer.

Size: 45cm (18").

Voice: male a non-descript rising wheezing noise, female a growling purr.

Habitat: vegetation cover at edges of streams, ponds and lakes.

Distribution: all year throughout Britain and Ireland; less common in the west.

Not to be confused with: the Wigeon (male has a pale forehead, off-white under parts, lavender breast, white forewing and green hindwing); and the Scaup (male has green-black head and white flanks).

24. **Goldfinch**

THE LATIN NAME FOR THE Goldfinch means "thistle", the bird's favourite in a mixed diet of ground plant and tree seeds, for which its small sharp bill is specially evolved. It makes a particularly comfortable nest in tree or shrub, of grass lined with lacy roots and soft cobwebs.

The Goldfinch is one of Britain's most striking small birds, with its almost oriental facemask and bright contrasting colour scheme. Large flocks of them – the collective noun is a charm – can be disturbed while feeding on patches of thistle in uncultivated ground, sending up a cloud of yellow and black wings.

It is presently undergoing something of a revival of fortune in Britain after it went into serious decline towards the end of the 20th century, with the loss of much of its traditional wasteland habitat to intensive farming and urban sprawl. The rural policy of encouraging "set-aside" – fields left uncultivated and ungrazed to permit the regeneration of wild flowers and the wildlife that feeds on them – has been very successful for the Goldfinch and other seed eaters thriving on weeds which would have been eradicated in a more "productive" field.

CARDUELIS CARDUELIS

Appearance: pale buff body with chestnut patches on breast; chestnut back; black cap on squat head; white cheeks and red mask with a black band enclosing bright black eyes; sharp pale triangular bill; black wings with bright yellow middle bar; black tail with white spots. Juvenile has grey-brown body and head.

Size: 12cm (5").

Voice: a tinkling t-lip t-lip chatter; song adds liquid trills.

Habitat: dry open ground with plenty of seeding weeds and bushes.

Distribution: all year throughout Ireland and Britain except northern Scotland and the western Isles.

Not to be confused with: the Greenfinch (Urban 1), slightly larger, greener all over and without the distinctive headmarkings; the Siskin (Urban 24), which has yellower back and all yellow face.

Chapter 4

The Urban
Habitat

BY DEFINITION THE URBAN habitat is an artificial one, a man-made environment whose very creation destroys the natural world. But nature reasserts itself at every opportunity. What looks like a church tower or an office block to you and me is just another rocky outcrop to the Peregrine; a boating pond in an ornamental park is no more or less than a welcome feeding pool to the Heron; a canal merely a different river to the Mallard in its reeds.

Some birds have been all too successful at adapting to mankind's world. The Feral Pigeon, direct descendent of the cliff-ledge resident Rock Dove, has felt perfectly at home on the ledge-like sills and pediments of buildings; it forages just as happily on the open spaces of Civic Park and Town Square as its relatives do on fields and open grassland. Along with Starlings and other species they are now regarded as a damaging and unhealthy pest – "a rat with feathers" – to be excluded by spikes and netting.

Suburban gardens have historically been a more conscious attempt by us humans to create a tame and manageable version of a wildlife habitat, the countryside. Although not to every bird's taste, a great many species have learned to tolerate such a level of intimacy with their human neighbours. After all, a hedge is a hedge whether it defines a garden or lines a

country lane. Many small birds have become quite dependent on the garden environment, particularly in winter when the increasing popularity of the bird table has been the saving of some species in particularly severe seasons.

The current trend for the garden to become an extension more of the house than of the countryside is having the opposite effect. Where hedges give way to painted panelling, lawns to decking and off-road parking, and ponds to patios and barbecue areas, many birds lose not only nesting opportunities but also food resources. The decline of the House Sparrow is much publicised, but it remains the commonest of garden birds; and populations of other regular garden visitors such as the Blackbird, the Blue Tit and the Greenfinch are all on the rise.

1. Greenfinch

A PERENNIAL FAVOURITE ON THE bird table, the Greenfinch is one of the commonest British finches, a successful resident not just here but throughout Europe. When feeding, Greenfinches gather together in huge loose flocks which swoop up in the air when disturbed.

The Greenfinch has the typical strong conical bill of all finches, a powerful tool for breaking open their diet of seeds. On the bird table its particular favourites are sunflower seeds,

hempseed and (unusual amongst British birds) buckwheat.

As well as the nuts and seeds they get from bird tables and elsewhere, the Greenfinch eats the young green shoots of new plant growth; and it is very happy to feed on bush fruits. In summer Greenfinch droppings and even their chins can be stained purple from a seasonal diet of blackberries.

The Greenfinch is a sociable bird happy to gather and feed with other finches and tits, although it may well squabble with them when competing for space at the table. It defends only a very small territory in the immediate vicinity of its nest.

CARDUELIS CHLORIS

Appearance: stocky yellow-green body with bright yellow flashes on wing and side of tail; grey patches on wing and cheek; strong pale pinky grey triangular bill. Female is more muted in colour; juvenile brown with buff streaks; male loses much of its colour in winter.

Size: 15cm (6").

Voice: a chattering ti-ti-ti-ti and a loud nasal soo-whee; song a mixture of the two with sharp musical trills.

Habitat: hedges, edge of woodland, gardens.

Distribution: all year throughout Britain and Ireland.

Not to be confused with: the Siskin (Urban 24), a smaller finch with pronounced black and yellow bars on wing and black cap on head; the female Crossbill has a passing similarity to the male Greenfinch with a greenish body and brownish wings, but a distinctive exaggerated hook on its upper bill.

2. Great Tit

A COLOURFUL AND WELCOME visitor in the garden, the Great Tit is a bit of a bruiser at the bird feeder. As the largest of the British tits, it can often be seen chasing off other birds who seek to share the nuts or seeds. In nature it tends to feed on or near the ground – it isn't as agile in flight as other tits, and can sometimes seem a little clumsy on the bird feeder.

The Great Tit is vulnerable to severe winters in the wild. During the unusually heavy snows of 1917-1918, for

example, up to 90% of their population perished. But in the last 50 years or so their numbers have actually increased, a result of the growing popularity over that period of bird tables and feeders.

Apart from its cheerfully repetitive two-tone sing-song, the Great Tit has around 50 recognisable calls, a large repertoire from a very vocal little bird.

As long as there are trees to nest in, the Great Tit is tolerant of a vast range of climate conditions; it is resident throughout Europe from Morocco to Lapland, from Ireland to Siberia.

PARUS MAJOR

Appearance: greeny yellow back; pale blue tail; pale grey-blue wings with white bar; yellow underparts with bold black stripe down the middle (bolder in the male); black head with white cheeks; thin black bill. Juvenile has duller colouring.

Size: 14cm (5").

Voice: wide repertoire of chinks, churrs and tsi-tsis; song is a simple tee-cha tee-cha sung in a variety of tones and accents.

Habitat: gardens, hedgerows, parks, woodland – anywhere with trees.

Distribution: all year throughout Britain and Ireland (less common in north west Scotland and the northern and western Isles).

Not to be confused with: the Coal Tit, a smaller bird with buff underparts, a grey back and a white patch on the back of the head); and the Blue Tit (Urban 3), which is also smaller, with a white head, black chin, black eye band and mid-blue cap.

3. **Blue Tit**

IF IT'S NOT TOO CONFUSING, the Blue Tit is Robin to the Great Tit's

Batman – smaller and with only a black eye-mask instead of the fuller black hood of the bigger bird. They are frequently in each other's company fighting with other diners for space at the bird table.

This is the chief culprit of doorstep crime, the bird that used to peck

PARUS CAERULEUS

Appearance: grey back above powder blue wings and tail (with a faint white bar on the wing); pale yellow underparts with a black central band between the legs; white head with a clear blue cap and black eye band; black on chin and back of neck; short thin black bill. Juvenile has all the same features but in an unkempt mousy brown over a yellow head and under parts.

Size: 11cm (4").

Voice: thin see-see-see-soo; also a rough churr like a Great Tit.

Habitat: gardens, parks and all wooded lands.

Distribution: all year throughout Britain and Ireland, but scarce in north west Scotland.

Not to be confused with: the Great Tit (Urban 2) which is larger, with a longer bill and a more predominantly black head; and the Coal Tit, of similar size, but with buff underparts, a grey back, black not blue cap, and a white patch on the back of the head.

through the foil on milk bottles to drink the cream. The Blue Tit is an agile visitor to bird feeders, often hanging upside down to peck at their contents. Away from the human environment it can be seen searching along the branches of trees for insects in the bark.

Blue Tits lay a large clutch of eggs, up to 16 of them. But the chicks are rather vulnerable in their first few weeks to predators such as cats and squirrels, and marauding birds like Magpies and Woodpeckers.

4. **Starling**

ALTHOUGH FACING A DECLINE in numbers at the moment, swarming flocks of Starlings are still a familiar sight in town and country. The Starling remains with the House Sparrow (also declining) the most populous bird in Britain. Smoky clouds of them in their hundreds of thousands move like solid objects through the evening sky, stretching and changing shape, and altering direction as one bird – a terrific display

of flying skill and group co-ordination.

In cities large Starling populations cause significant defacement and even damage to buildings. Limestone is particularly vulnerable to erosion by the high acidity of their droppings.

The Starling's talent for mimicry was

STURNUS VULGARIS

Appearance: shiny black body with iridescent purple and green; short square tail, thick pink-brown legs and feet; squat head with black eye; sharp yellow bill with base of blue (males) or pink (females). In winter, iridescence fades to reveal a dark brown body with large white spots and bill also turns darker. Juveniles have plain mid-brown body and dark bill.

Size: 21cm (8").

Voice: characteristic falling whistled whee-oo and rasping cha-ar; but has a huge range of notes and noises, and is also known to mimic other birds.

Habitat: forestry, man-made structures (bridges, piers etc.).

Distribution: all year throughout Britain and Ireland – summer only in north west Scotland.

Not to be confused with: the male Blackbird (Urban 5) with its slightly larger plain black body, longer tail and all-yellow bill; the Blackbird also hops, whereas the Starling walks.

noted by Shakespeare, who wrote of it in his play Henry IV Part 1. In 1890 an enthusiast, attempting to introduce to America all the birds named in Shakespeare's works, released the first 80 Starlings in New York's Central Park. By a twist of chance the first reported nesting site was on the city's Museum of Natural History! 116 years later, the North American population now numbers over 200 million, a third of the entire world population of the bird and a major threat to native American species.

5. **Blackbird**

THE BLACKBIRD'S SUPREMELY musical song forms the core of the dawn chorus. Creatures of habit, they often sing from the same perch, so with patience you may get to recognise individual birds and their voices.

The sight of a Blackbird feeding is familiar – hopping rather than walking – as it roots about in short grass or leaf litter for worms, bugs, and grubs – and shows the bird's origins as a woodland species which has adapted well to the man-mown environment. It is a member of the extensive thrush family, which also includes the Robin, the Nightingale, the Stonechat and the Wheatear. Birds of great variety in size, plumage and song, they all share a preference for woodland habitat and ground-feeding.

Traditionally a girl could tell what sort of man she would marry by the first bird she saw on St Valentine's Day. A Blackbird signified that her husband would be a priest; a Robin meant a sailor, a Sparrow a farmer, a Crossbill a quarreller, a Dove a good man, any yellow bird a wealthy man, any blue bird a happy one, and a Woodpecker meant marrying no man at all.

TURDUS MERULA

Appearance: male has all-black body, dark legs and striking yellow eye-ring round black eye. Female is dark brown with slightly paler underparts and indistinct dark brown spotted mottling and paler legs; both have bright yellow bill. Juvenile is a paler brown.

Size: 25cm (10").

Voice: a joyous full-throated musical warble ending with a few faster scratchy notes.

Habitat: gardens, hedgerows, woodland.

Distribution: all year throughout Britain and Ireland.

Not to be confused with: the Starling (Urban 4), which in both its black and its brown plumage is smaller and stockier with paler legs; the Ring Ouzel (a summer visitor to Britain) a similar but smaller black bird but with a prominent white breast; and the Song Thrush (Urban 7) and Mistle Thrush (Urban 23), both similar to the female Blackbird but with paler brown underparts showing off the dark brown spotting more clearly.

6. Black-Headed Gull

THE BLACK-HEADED GULL IS NOT very well named – for a start the head is chocolate brown, not black, and indeed for much of the year it is a blotchy white. As a seagull, it's as likely to be found inland as anywhere near the sea! The Black-Headed Gull has forged an extremely successful partnership with mankind, making the most of our waterworks, disused quarries and throw-away culture.

It nests in vast noisy colonies by any stretch of open water from lochs to flooded gravel pits, where the sound of their incessant chatter, especially when disturbed, can be quite deafening. Animated clouds of Black-Headed Gulls will often be seen trailing like exhaust fumes behind a ploughing tractor in late summer, searching for unearthed worms and grubs.

LARUS RIDIBUNDUS

Appearance: white body with very pale grey back; very dark brown mask from chin to crown on otherwise white head; dark red bill and legs; pale grey wings with white front edge at outer wing and black trailing edge at tips. In winter the mask fades to little more than a dark ear, and bill and legs fade to a bright orange.

Size: 36cm (14").

Voice: very noisy rasping laugh of kwar-kwar.

Habitat: town and country, inland and coastal, from reservoir to rubbish tip.

Distribution: all year throughout Britain and Ireland, not quite as common inland in the south.

Not to be confused with: the Mediterranean Gull which has a fuller black hood and a thicker bill, with white not black wing tips; and the Common Gull, slightly larger, with yellow bill and legs, white head and darker grey body; the Little Gull is much smaller and generally confined to the coast, with a black hood and all-black bill.

7. Song Thrush

THE SONG THRUSH OFTEN JOINS the dawn chorus, generally once the Blackbirds, Robins and even Wrens have been at it for a while! Although it sings all year round, it really starts in earnest from late winter onwards – the Thrush raises two or three broods a year, from March to August. As the summer wears on, harsher notes creep into the bird's repertoire, as if the Thrush were losing its voice a little after singing so long and beautifully.

Thrushes feed on worms and slugs, as well as berries and other fruit – they are a common sight in orchards, pecking at rotting windfalls in search of seeds.

TURDUS PHILOMELOS

Appearance: mid to dark brown upper parts; pale buff underparts, yellower towards face, with clear dark brown spots; a dark streak below the cheek; black eye with pale eye-ring; in flight, pale orange underwing revealed; black upper bill, yellow lower; in song, orange yellow mouth revealed.

Size: 23cm (9").

Voice: short clear whistled notes in short phrases repeated three or four times; mostly musical, with some harsher sounds.

Habitat: woodland, hedgerow and shrubbery.

Distribution: all year throughout Britain and Ireland.

Not to be confused with: the Mistle Thrush (Urban 23) a larger bird with bolder darker spots, greyer-brown upper parts and a more slender neck; the female Blackbird (Urban 5) a larger bird with all-yellow bill, whose darker upper body and underparts make the dark brown spots much less distinguishable.

When the ground gets too hard to pull worms from, the Thrush will eat snails, and you may be lucky enough to find a Thrush's anvil – a convenient stone on which the bird hammers the snail-shells like a blacksmith to get at the food inside. Sometimes you may catch a Blackbird sneaking in to steal the snail after the Thrush has been so kind as to break it open.

8. **Robin**

A TRADITION GOING BACK TO Elizabethan times says that the Robin covered the dead with leaves. The Robin is supposed to have got its red breast from having plucked a thorn from Jesus' crown and been splashed with his blood. Another version says it was scorched red taking dew-water into Hell to give to sinners.

Robins were also used to predict country weather – to see one sing deep in the shelter of a tree meant rain was on the way, but if it sang on an exposed outer branch the weather would be fine.

Robins can be very tame in the presence of man. A familiar red breast will often appear in the garden as soon as you start digging, in the hope of picking up any freshly unearthed grubs and beetles. They have been known to take live bait from the hands

of anglers.

Like all members of the thrush family, Robins tend to feed on the ground – the Robin will tolerate an open bird table but is not keen on one with a roof and very rarely attempts to hang from a bird feeder.

ERITHACUS RUBECULA

Appearance: compact round bird. Brown upper parts, mid-buff underside; unmistakable bright red breast and face; mid-grey patches either side of breast and neck; white patch below chest; bright black eye with pale yellow eye-ring; short thin dark bill. Juvenile has mottled brown all over, from which the adult's red features emerge first as red spots.

Size: 14cm (5").

Voice: short ticks and seeps and longer musical phrases.

Habitat: woodland, parks and gardens.

Distribution: all year throughout Britain and Ireland.

Not to be confused with: the Dunnock (Urban 17), all-brown like the juvenile Robin but with greyer throat and under parts, brown eyes and with black streaks to the wings; the Stonechat (Country 11) has a duller red breast and no red on the face, and although the female Stonechat's upper parts are a similar brown, the male's are quite black.

9. **Wren**

IT SEEMS IMPOSSIBLE THAT THE giant voice of the Wren should come out of such a small body, and the little bird quivers from tail to bill as it forces its song out to fill the air.

The tiny Wren is extremely vulnerable to severe winters, but unlike other species seems to be able to recover its numbers very quickly. This may be explained by the fact that many of the species are polygamous.

In a well-known folk tale the Wren was crowned king of the birds in a flying contest because it clung onto the back of the eagle and therefore flew the highest.

St Stephen's feast day is Boxing Day, and in former times was an occasion for hunting and stoning Wrens; a Wren is supposed to have betrayed the saint by singing from the bush where he was hiding. In the past, 26th December was even known as Wrenning Day.

The Latin name, Troglodytes, means cave-dweller. The Wren is so named because it builds its nest in dark, damp places – under hedges, for example, or in crevices in cliffs. The British Wren is the only species of the Wren family to live outside North America, and has prospered in Europe because of the lack of competition from other Wren species that it faces "back home".

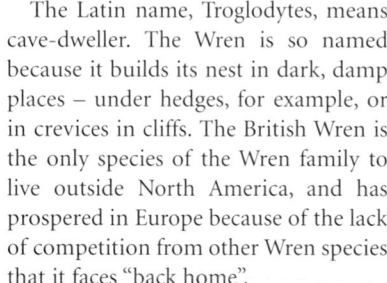

TROGLODYTES TROGLODYTES

Appearance: small brown bird. Mid-brown upper parts, buff chest, cream throat and no neck; cream eyebrow over bright black eye; very short up-turned tail; fine black barring on wings, with white bars on black wingtips; relatively long sharp bill, black above and yellow beneath.

Size: 9cm (3").

Voice: incredibly loud full-throated short bursts of warbling and trills; alarm call is a sharp chik-chik-chik.

Habitat: everywhere from gardens to mountainsides, from woodland to open heath.

Distribution: all year throughout Britain and Ireland.

Not to be confused with: the Dunnock (Urban 17), which has a grey not cream throat, and faint grey collar; the juvenile Robin (Urban 8) is larger, with red spots and not black bars.

10. Collared Dove

THE COLLARED DOVE HAS TAKEN advantage of man-made habitats to

STREPTOPELIA DECAOCTA

Appearance: pale brown body; long darker brown tail with white tip; thin black half-collar round back of neck; light pink breast and small light pink head; dark eye with a white eye-ring; red legs; dark wing tips. Juvenile is all brown with no collar.

Size: 32cm (13").

Voice: repetitive coo-COO-coo; in flight a nasal wheezing whurr.

Habitat: farms, gardens and parkland, especially in coniferous trees.

Distribution: all year throughout Britain and Ireland.

Not to be confused with: the Feral Pigeon (Urban 13), slightly stockier, dark grey with no collar and a distinctive white spot on bridge of bill; the Woodpigeon (Country 3) much larger and stockier with dark grey back and distinguishing white patches either side of neck instead of black collar; the Turtle Dove is significantly smaller with a richer mottled brown and orange back and wings and reddish eyes – it is only a summer visitor to Britain, and rare north of Yorkshire.

achieve a quite astonishing expansion to its range. Spreading from Asia into the Balkans no earlier than the 1930s, the first pair bred in Britain as recently as 1955. Yet now the species is a common resident throughout Europe (except Spain and the Alps) and southern Scandinavia and Russia, with the British population alone in excess of 200,000.

It owes its success to its opportunism, taking full advantage of food and scraps left out accidentally by people. Its phenomenal spread has also been helped by the fact that it breeds throughout the year, producing as many as four two-egg clutches a year. (So in a lifespan of up to 10 years, a pair of Collared Doves might produce over 60 offspring!)

Particularly fond of grain, it can often be seen on farmland, or on bird tables muscling in on seed put out for smaller birds. The Collared Dove is unique amongst British pigeons and doves in calling during flight.

11. House Martin

THE HOUSE MARTIN BUILDS A characteristic enclosed nest of mud pellets with an entrance on top, stuck high up on buildings underneath overhanging beams and roofs. As flocks gather in great numbers in the autumn before their return migration to Africa, they can be seen perched on wires in packed rows like an expectant audience.

Because House Martins build and perch on such man-made structures they have a reputation for close association with man, but in fact have no real interaction with us – for example they

DELICHON URBICA

Appearance: white underparts and stocky white feathered legs; blue-black back and hood above a white throat; a distinguishing white rump (not always visible in flight), with a short, forked, dark tail; upper wing brown-black, underwing dark grey to rear and paler grey to fore.

Size: 13cm (5").

Voice: a clipped chirrit; song a fast musical twittering with trills.

Habitat: buildings of town and country, and occasionally natural cliffs.

Distribution: March to October throughout Britain and Ireland, less common in northernmost Scotland.

Not to be confused with: the Sand Martin which has a dark not white rump and deep sandy brown upper parts; the Swift, a larger all-dark bird which does not share the House Martin's perching habit; the Swallow (Country 12) has a red throat, more pronounced blue in its upper parts, no white rump and a much deeper longer forked tail.

never visit the garden for food, feeding strictly on the wing.

Flight is a good way to distinguish the House Martin from other aerial feeders such as the Swift and Swallow. Where the Swift darts about, and the Swallow has a twisting dive, the House Martin seems to float through the air with fluttering sails for wings.

Time of sighting may also be a useful indicator: as a rule these insect-catching migrants arrive between late March and late April in the following order: Sand Martin, Swallow, House Martin, Swift.

12. **Chaffinch**

AMONG THE COMMONEST BRITISH garden birds, the Chaffinch is a frequent and numerous visitor to the bird table, beneath which it hops about on the ground looking for fallen seeds.

The Swedish botanist Carl von Linne, who invented the two-part Latin naming system for all plants and animals in the 18th century, gave the Chaffinch the

name coelebs, which means "bachelor". He had noticed that it was mainly female Chaffinches who migrate from Sweden to swell the British population in winter, leaving the males at home and alone. Happily for all concerned, British Chaffinches both male and female live here all year round.

The Brambling, another winter migrant to all but northern Britain and western Ireland from its breeding grounds in northern and eastern Europe, is a close relative of the Chaffinch and the two often feed together. So the winter bird table presents a good opportunity to spot the differences between them.

FRINGILLA COELEBS

Appearance: male has brown back; pale pink underside merging to white at tail; deep pink-brown face and chest; blue-grey bill and top and back of head, with darker patch just above bill; dark brown wings with two white bars. Female is generally duller, more grey-brown all over, but retains the white wing bars.

Size: 15cm (6").

Voice: a bright insistent pink-pink; song a cheerful chi-chi-chi-chi-chi-chip chi-whee-oo.

Habitat: woodlands, parks and gardens.

Distribution: all year throughout Britain and Ireland.

Not to be confused with: the Brambling which has similar wing marks but a yellow bill, darker mottled back and head, more orangey chest and bright white rump and under parts; the female House Sparrow (Urban 16), similar in size to the female Chaffinch but lacks the distinguishing white bars on the wings; the Bullfinch shares the pink breast of the Chaffinch but has an unmistakable shallow black head, and black wings.

13. **Feral Pigeon**

THE FERAL, OR TOWN, PIGEON IS A direct descendant of the Rock Dove, itself now quite a rare coastal resident in its pure form. The feral cousin is ubiquitous in Britain's towns and cities, where it displays a bewildering variation in plumage as a result of long interbreeding with other species.

Living to an age of up to 35 years in captivity (although more usually around 15) the Town Pigeon often survives only 5 in the harsh urban environment. It has adapted well to a diet of discarded human food, perhaps because it has only 37 taste buds, compared to human beings' 10,000!

Beloved of tourists from Venice to Trafalgar Square and hated by those responsible for the upkeep of public buildings, the Feral Pigeon is undeniably a messy bird whose droppings and scruffy nests do much to deface the urban environment.

More positively it has learnt very successfully to live alongside humans, and for many a small child with a bag of bread crumbs the Feral Pigeon will be his or her first close encounter with the bird world.

SAXICOLA TORQUATA

Appearance: huge variations because of inter-breeding with other pigeon and dove species; generally dark grey body and head with lighter grey belly and darker tail and wingtips; red eye with white eye-ring; red legs and feet; green and pink iridescence around neck and chest; large white spot on nose.

Size: 33cm (13").

Voice: repeated classic purring hoo-hoo-hoo-HOO-rr.

Habitat: ledges anywhere, from cliff to city centre.

Distribution: all year throughout Britain and Ireland.

Not to be confused with: the Rock Dove, which has a much smaller white dot on the nose, and a light grey back and wings with bold black wingbars; the Stock Dove, with a darker belly, fainter wingbars and more pronounced iridescence; and the Woodpigeon (Country 3), a much bigger bird with distinctive white patches on either side of the neck and a bold pink-grey breast.

14. Moorhen

THE MOORHEN'S LONG GREEN-yellow toes, not webbed but spread wide, are a development enabling it to stalk on very wet land, browsing for food, without sinking down. Although the Moorhen does swim, it is not comfortable on open water. In flight the bright legs trail behind the bird, giving a flash of the red garter band and the splash of white beneath the tail.

Demonstrating another use for their unusual feet, female Moorhens can be seen during the breeding season fighting each other on the water by kicking out forwards with them as they compete for males.

The bird's name is a corruption of merehen or mirehen – the mire or marsh is after all the bird's true habitat, not the moor. The name may have evolved in reference to its dark colouring – Elizabethans referred to any dark-skinned men as Moors (although the name only accurately applied to Moroccans).

Other names for the Moorhen include Cuddy (in Scotland), Stankhen or Stankie (after stank, a pond with little or no flowing water), and Skitty (referring to its skittish, apparently random walk).

GALLINULA CHLOROPUS

Appearance: body and head dark brown-black all over, with bold white under tail; white line along side; yellow tip on red bill, which extends back to forehead as a red shield; dark red eye; greeny yellow legs with red band above knee and large widely splayed feet. Juvenile has brown body and all-yellow bill.

Size: 33cm (13").

Voice: sudden metallic warning currack, or a rattled huck-huck-huck-huck.

Habitat: damp undergrowth beside or near ponds, rivers and other fresh water.

Distribution: all year throughout Ireland and Britain except north west Scotland.

Not to be confused with: the Coot (Urban 15) which has a larger blacker body, and white shield running into all-white bill; and the Water Rail, a smaller waterside resident with mid-brown back streaked with darker brown, grey-buff underparts, pink legs and long thin red bill with black tip.

15. **Coot**

A VERY SHOWY BIRD, THE COOT raises its body feathers in a territorial display to warn off rivals and predators, and if that doesn't work will sometimes engage in fighting, using bill as well as feet. Its awkward take-off on water, paddling across the surface like a Swan, may also have served the purpose of making a noisy demonstration of its presence.

Coots are sociable birds, feeding together in large groups or "covers" on ponds. They dive to depths of up to 2m (6ft) in search of larvae, also eating

FULICA ATRA

Appearance: all-black body and head; white bill extending back to forehead as a white shield; red eye; green legs with long-toed grey feet; flight reveals a pale hind-edge to wings.

Size: 37cm (14").

Voice: abrupt culk in alarm, and a chatty cu-cu-cu.

Habitat: reeds and other waterside vegetation by lakes, larger ponds and slower rivers than the Moorhen.

Distribution: all year throughout Ireland and Britain except north west Scotland.

Not to be confused with: the Moorhen (Urban 14), which is slightly smaller with a browner body and a splash of white under the tail, and a red shield leading to red and yellow bill; the Moorhen has green not grey feet and prefers a more intimate environment than the Coot.

weeds and seeds. Very rarely, Coots drown after getting their bills trapped, for example in trying to open a freshwater mussel. This has given rise to the romantic myth that badly injured Coots dive in order to die underwater, anchoring themselves by their bills to deep weeds.

The phrase "bald as a Coot" refers to the white shield on the forehead, which looks like bare skin in the midst of the black head. This may also relate to the origins of the bird's name – in German, "Kutte" means a monk's habit, so perhaps the apparently bald patch made its early observers think of a monk's tonsure. When it walks the Coot looks like a stooped old man with his hands behind his back, hence the expression "silly old coot".

16. House Sparrow

THIS IS THE ARCHETYPAL "LITTLE brown bird", and its close association with human habitation means that it is correspondingly less common in more sparsely populated parts of the country such as the Scottish Highlands. The sharp decline in House Sparrow population across most of western Europe has been a cause for concern – 64% of the British population has disappeared in the last 25 years, although it

PASSER DOMESTICUS

Appearance: little brown bird. Male has grey underside; black streaks on brown back, with darker tail; grey cap; black eye stripe and chin, both running from thickset black bill; white wingbar. Female has grey-buff under parts; brown cap; pale brown eyebrow running back from eye; no white wingbar.

Size: 14cm (5").

Voice: a much repeated cheerful chirrup, sometimes runs together with other chips and chirps to make a full song with trills.

Habitat: roof spaces and other cavities in or near human habitation.

Distribution: all year throughout Britain and Ireland.

Not to be confused with: the Tree Sparrow (absent from western Ireland, Wales, western England and most of Scotland) which has a white collar, less distinct white wingbar and reddish brown cap; and the Dunnock (Urban 17) which has a much slimmer bill, all-brown head, no black eye stripe or chin and a finer white wingbar.

is still (with the Starling) the most common British garden bird.

Its successful relationship with mankind may be shown in the fact that it was unknown in North America until a few pairs were released in New York's Central Park in 1850 – it is now one of the commonest birds on the continent.

Although known and named for building its nests in buildings, the House Sparrow has also been known to build within the structures of other birds including the Rook, the House Martin and the Magpie.

17. **Dunnock**

(also called HEDGE SPARROW)

THE DUNNOCK PREFERS TO FEED on the ground, never far from cover, often on whatever has fallen from the bird table. Easily overlooked in its featureless plumage and unremarkable song, it is nevertheless one of the commonest of garden birds.

If for nothing else, it is notable for its mating habits. It forms threesomes – two males and a female or vice versa – perhaps in an instinctive attempt to maximise its fertility.

The Dunnock is also known as the Hedge Accentor – the accentor family of birds occur only in the Old World territories of Europe, northern Africa and Asia. Of the 12 species, only two breed in Europe: the Dunnock, and the Alpine Accentor which, as its name suggests, only occurs in a band through the Alps from northern Spain to the Black Sea. The Alpine is a broadly grey bird, with dark brown streaks above and reddish brown streaks below, a familiar sight in ski resorts where it scavenges for crumbs at mountain-top cafes.

PRUNELLA MODULARIS

Appearance: little brown bird. Mid-brown back with dark brown streaks; neat brown tail; faint white wingbar revealed in flight; grey-buff underparts; grey throat and faint grey collar; grey brown cap above brown eye and brown cheek; thin black bill; fragile orange-brown legs. Juvenile has mottled brown and grey under parts.

Size: 14cm (5").

Voice: soft to hard pleading sip-sip-sip; song an unimaginative flat warble.

Habitat: shrubbery and hedgerows, woodland undergrowth, overgrown heath.

Distribution: all year throughout Britain and Ireland except Shetland.

Not to be confused with: the Wren (Urban 9), a smaller bird with a short tail, clear fine barring on the back and wings and a buff throat, face and eyebrow; the female House Sparrow (Urban 16) has a much thicker bill and less grey underparts; the juvenile Robin (Urban 8) has reddish spots on its back and head.

18. **Fieldfare**

FIELDFARES ARE WINTER VISITORS to our shores, from northern Scandinavia and Russia. Forming large

TURDUS PILARIS

Appearance: dark brown back with slightly paler speckle; black tail and steel grey rump; off-white belly merging to pale orange throat, all with black V-shaped spots; bright yellow bill blackened at tip; black eye with yellow eye-ring, in steel grey head; dark line below cheek. In flight the underwing is revealed as largely white.

Size: 25cm (10").

Voice: a loud, chuckling check-check-check; the song is a musically weak mix of whistles and squeaks.

Habitat: open woodland, maturely hedged pasture, orchards.

Distribution: October to March, through-out Britain and Ireland.

Not to be confused with: the slightly larger Mistle Thrush (Urban 23) which has a yellower belly and paler brown upper parts without the grey head and rump; the slightly smaller Song Thrush ((Urban 7) which also lacks the grey head colour and is buff not white underwing in flight; the Kestrel (Country 8), with similar although slightly paler markings, is nevertheless a much larger bird with a very different habit.

loose flocks they roam the countryside looking for insects on the ground and winter fruit from tree and bush.

Like our other winter-visiting thrush the Redwing, the Fieldfare has in places become resident with a few pairs now breeding in the harsher climate of the Scottish Highlands where it can feel at home.

Migrating Fieldfares do not return to the same destination every year; there are reports of the same bird that wintered in one location turning up 1000 miles away the next year. But this flexible approach may be the saving of the Fieldfare, allow-ing it to head for milder areas during severe winters. For example during a vicious frost lasting 59 days in the winter of 1890-91, Fieldfares which had migrated to Norfolk left the country again. By the same token, extra birds may arrive in Britain if the con-tinental winter is unusually harsh.

19. **Redwing**

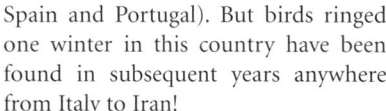

IN HARSHER WINTERS THE Redwing may stray into quiet parks and large gardens. But generally it keeps itself to itself, breeding and feeding in small groups away from human habitation except in extreme conditions. They can be seen in loose groups grazing for worms in fields, or feasting on berries in hedgerows.

Redwings travel in flocks, often mixed with Fieldfares (the other thrush to come to Britain as a winter visitor). The red wings of the former and the grey heads of the latter make them easily distinguishable.

The Redwing is as erratic a migrant as the Fieldfare, most unpredictable in returning to the same area. Generally Icelandic birds come to Scotland and Ireland, Scandinavian birds to England (sometimes stopping, sometimes en route for Spain and Portugal). But birds ringed one winter in this country have been found in subsequent years anywhere from Italy to Iran!

In recent years some Redwing and Fieldfare have begun to live and breed in the north of Scotland, where the rugged climate and extensive forestry presumably remind it of its native Scandinavian or Icelandic homelands.

TURDUS ILIACUS

Appearance: olive-brown back, pale underparts speckled with dark spots (unspotted at tail); striking rust-red underwing visible even at rest; olive-brown head with bold cream stripes over eye and under cheek; sharp yellow bill, black towards tip; pink legs.

Size: 21cm (8").

Voice: high thin seep; song a short repeated flute-like phrase.

Habitat: mature pasture, open woodland, bushy heathland.

Distribution: October to May throughout Britain and Ireland; all year in northern Scotland.

Not to be confused with: the Song Thrush (Urban 7), slightly larger, similarly coloured but without the creamy head stripes or of course the red underwing; the Fieldfare (Urban 18) also lacks the red underwing, and has a grey head, with more pronounced dark spots on underparts.

20. **Mallard**

Appearance: male has pale grey-brown body with chocolate brown breast and neck; white neck ring below bottle-green head; yellow bill. Both sexes have distinctive broad petrol-blue hindwing, with thin white stripe behind and in front of the blue. The female has orange-brown bill and white tail; otherwise a typically plain brown mottled brown and white female duck.

Size: 60cm (24").

Voice: classic single quack; male is quieter, with an occasional soft wheezing whistle in display.

Habitat: almost any water, from marsh to lake from park pond to river.

Distribution: all year throughout Britain and Ireland.

Not to be confused with: the male Shoveler (Country 17), Teal (Country 22) and Scaup, all of which have green head markings; but the Scaup has a black breast and white flanks, the Shoveler a white breast and black and longer bill, and the Teal only a green eye patch on an otherwise chocolate brown head. Female ducks are much harder to separate; the Shoveler (Country 17) has a much longer bill, the Gadwall an orange bill, white wing patch and no white on the tail, the Pintail a grey bill, and the Teal (Country 22) is almost half the size of the Mallard; none have the blue hindwing of the female Mallard.

LIKE A GREAT MANY BIRDS THE male Mallard looks its finest during the winter courting season. As summer wears on it moults and becomes a more muted brown – even its classic green head seems muddy and bedraggled. At its best it is the most easily recognised and attractive of our British ducks.

The Mallard feeds by dabbling – up-ending itself on the water, tail in the air, to grope below the surface for weeds and insects.

The domestic farmyard duck is a direct descendant which closely resembles the Mallard. In addition to the genuinely wild bird, many Mallards are bred in captivity and released for shooting.

21. **Mute Swan**

MALE SWANS ARE CALLED COBS, females are known as pens, and young birds are cygnets. Once hunted for their meat, Swans are now welcomed as a beautiful sight on public waterways. Swans are majestic in flight, with their slow, powerful wing beats, and on water, the long take-off and controlled landing are impressive sights.

A Swan can be quite tame, accepting food from humans at times. But it is wise to approach the bird with caution; when alarmed, particularly at breeding times, Swans can become aggressive, arching their wings and lowering their necks in attack with a threatening hiss.

In ancient Greek legend the soul of Apollo, the god of music, entered a Swan. This gave rise to the notion that the best poets' souls inhabited swans after their deaths. Shakespeare, for example, is known as the Swan of Avon. The myth that Swans sing beautifully before they die gave rise to the idea of a swan-song as a last great work by a performer or writer.

In medieval times the British Crown claimed ownership of all Mute Swans as a valuable food for banquets. To this day an annual pageant, know as swan-upping, takes place on the Thames, in which some Swans are ceremonially marked by the Queen's Swan Marker.

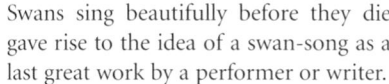

CYGNUS OLOR

Appearance: large all-white body; long wedge-shaped tail; short black leathery legs and webbed feet; long muscular neck sometimes off-white; orange bill with black tip and black knob at face; black face forward of eyes. Juvenile has grey-brown plumage and dark grey bill, which gradually adopt adult colouring.

Size: 150cm (60").

Voice: hisses and grunts aggressively when threatened.

Habitat: larger ponds, rivers, lakes and reservoirs.

Distribution: all year throughout Britain and Ireland, but less common in the far north.

Not to be confused with: the Whooper Swan and Bewick's Swan, both winter-only visitors to Britain, and both with yellow not orange bills; Bewick's Swan is also much smaller.

22. **Blackcap**

YOUR EARS WILL PROBABLY notice the Blackcap before you see it. Unremarkable in plumage, it has the most musical of songs. Like other members of the warbler family, it is an insect eater in the summer, and readily

---

SYLVIA ATRICAPILLA

Appearance: male has grey-brown back, paler grey underparts, mid to dark grey neck and face; dark eye with thin white line on lower rim; small black cap; fine dark grey bill. Female has brown back and buff underparts, with rusty brown cap.

Size: 14cm (5").

Voice: hard staccato tak; song a short, fast warble of high, bright notes rising in volume and confidence.

Habitat: woodland undergrowth, larger gardens.

Distribution: all year in southern Ireland and Britain, a summer migrant further north, unusual in northern Scotland.

Not to be confused with: the male resembles the Marsh Tit and the Willow Tit, but both those are smaller, with buff-brown underparts, white cheeks, black chins and larger caps; the female is similar to the Garden Warbler, which however has a richer buff underside, shorter bill and no cap.

---

moves on to fruit at the end of the breeding season. The Blackcap is fond of wild berries such as elder and honeysuckle, and is happy to come to the bird table in winter, with a particular weakness for balls of fat containing seeds or dried insects.

It shares a similar range, habitat and even song with its cousin the Garden Warbler (the Garden Warbler's song is slightly longer and lower in pitch). The main difference in habit is the end of season moult – the Blackcap moults completely before heading south for northern Africa, whereas the Garden Warbler waits until he has arrived. As British and northern and eastern European Blackcaps leave for Africa, some mid-European Blackcaps migrate the shorter distances to Britain or the Mediterranean.

23. **Mistle Thrush**

THE MISTLE AND SONG THRUSHES are distinguishable by size, plumage and song, and also by their flight when disturbed. The Song Thrush tends to fly off a short distance at low level, while the Mistle Thrush generally flies much higher and further away.

The Mistle Thrush breeds (and therefore sings) earlier in the year than other thrushes, starting as early as February and producing two or three broods in the course of the year.

The Mistle Thrush is an aggressive protector of its territory, and will defend its claim to a well-berried bush with a furious football-rattle alarm and a proud upright stance. It gets its name from its taste for feeding on mistletoe berries in the winter. In summer, it's equally happy hopping along the ground in search of worms and seeds. It is known in some parts of the countryside as the Stormcock, from its habit of singing from treetops in wild weather.

TURDUS VISCIVORUS

Appearance: grey-brown upper parts; thin white edges to tail; creamy buff underparts with large dark brown spots; slim neck and small head with speckled brown and off-white face; large dark eye in white eye-ring; flight reveals pale brown rump and white underwing; upper legs white-feathered, lower legs pink.

Size: 27cm (10").

Voice: loud, sweet, melancholy whistled song, faster than Blackbird, less repetitive than Song Thrush; alarm call of fast rattling chatter.

Habitat: parkland, open mature woodland, orchards and large gardens.

Distribution: All year throughout Ireland and Britain except the western and northern Isles.

Not to be confused with: the Song Thrush (Urban 7) a slightly smaller bird with a richer brown back, orange-buff underwing, smaller spots on the underside, a stockier head and a more repetitive song ; the Fieldfare (Urban 18) differs with a grey head, darker tail, cream chin, orange-buff breast and yellow bill.

24. **Siskin**

THE SISKIN IS OFTEN SEEN IN THE company of Redpolls, with whom it shares both breeding and winter habitats. In addition to its regular diet of tree seeds, it has in recent years

CARDUELIS SPINUS

Appearance: green-yellow back and head; black wings with bold yellow bar; yellow rump and tail with bold inverted black T at tip; speckled whitish belly; yellowish breast; yellow cheeks and eye stripe; black chin and cap; quite thick pale bill. Female is less yellow, more grey-brown in tone, has whiter belly and no black cap.

Size: 12cm (5").

Voice: tinny whistled see-you or soo-weet; song a twittering of notes ending in a buzzing dge-dge-dgee.

Habitat: conifer forestry; in winter alder, birch and larch along rivers.

Distribution: all year in pockets in north and west Britain and Ireland; elsewhere a winter visitor.

Not to be confused with: the Greenfinch (Urban 1) a much larger finch with an even stubbier bill, plain olive-brown belly and no black cap; the female is a little like the female Redpoll, but without the latter's prominent red forehead.

acquired a taste for bird table food, in particular red peanuts.

It has a striking display flight in which it will circle above the trees with fluffed up plumage singing an energetic medley of warbles, wheezes and trills.

The Siskin is a welcome success story among British birds. 40 years ago it was relatively rare, a Scottish resident with English and Welsh outposts. The development of the conifer forestry industry throughout Britain and Ireland has enabled the Siskin to expand its breeding range in the summer.

In winter, the increasing popularity of bird tables has allowed the Siskin to remain in areas after it has exhausted the local supply of tree seeds. At the same time European birds have begun to winter in Britain, further swelling the population.

Chapter 5

The Coastal Habitat

NOTHING DEFINES BRITAIN MORE in every sense than its coastline. We are an island: our whole history as a nation is bound up in it. Our climate is dictated by our setting in the seas, bathed from the south and west by the warm Gulf Stream and from the north and east by the cold Arctic air. The historical accidents of our geology have created a variety of coastal conditions unique in the world, with a wildlife population to match.

The mineral-rich mudflats of our wide river estuaries and the distinctive flora of the saltmarshes, the sheltered settings of our gently sloping sand and shingle beaches, the aerial fortresses of our cliffs and the moated castles of the offshore islands – they all offer distinct and special advantages to the birds that choose to inhabit them.

The coastal habitat offers nesting sites of every kind for breeding birds – cliff ledges for the Kittiwake, sandy slopes for the burrowing Puffin, marsh grasses to hide the waders' shallow nest-scoops, offshore rocks to keep the predators at bay.

Other birds are attracted by the dietary variety which the meeting of land and sea allows. It's not just the fish – rocky foreshores support a varied menu of crustacean life, and both mudflats and intertidal sands contain rich communities of invertebrates. Mankind's mark at the seaside should

not be underestimated as a source of food for our coastal birds, be they the Herring Gulls scavenging the rubbish tip or the Fulmars following the fishing fleets for scraps and waste.

Britain's temperate climate is a particular attraction for migrating seabirds. They might be fleeing the extremities of winter in their breeding grounds further north, like the Turnstone; or coming to land only to breed in our relatively safe inshore environment before returning to more open ocean waters like the members of the auk family. This mix of transient and permanent residents makes the coastal habitat a thrilling one for the birdwatcher, a scene of constant change, renewal and surprise.

1. **Curlew**

NATURALLY SHARING A HABITAT with other waders, the Curlew is easy to identify as it feeds amongst them by the graceful curve of its bill, obvious both in flight and on the ground.

Although the Curlew is a British resident species, it is also a migrant: Scottish Curlews migrate to Ireland and the west coast of Britain, while those found on the east coast have travelled from Scandinavia and eastern Europe.

The Curlew is also significantly larger

and more widespread than any other British waders. As well as the call from which it gets its name, it has a beautiful display song, a bubbling, liquid trill hauntingly familiar to walkers on moors at breeding time, where it seems to spring from all directions as one

bird after another takes it up.

An Irish country tradition says that when the Curlew gives a double whistle, rain is on the way – a useful warning for walkers! In England sailors were warned not to go to sea if they heard a Curlew calling while flying overhead.

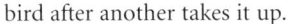

NUMENIUS ARQUATA

Appearance: long grey legs; white belly and rump; speckled sandy brown breast, back and head; darker speckled brown back; dark eye in cream eye-ring; distinctive very long bill curving slightly downwards.

Size: 55cm (22").

Voice: accelerating crescendo of coor-coor-coor; repetitious cur-lee; in alarm cu-cu-cu-cu.

Habitat: summer wetlands of moor, meadow and marsh; winter estuaries and coastal shores.

Distribution: all year throughout Britain and Ireland, more commonly in the north and west.

Not to be confused with: several smaller waders, especially the Whimbrel, a much less common summer visitor, mostly to the far north and Scottish islands, with a sharper bend to its bill and indistinct dark strips on its crown; the Bar-Tailed Godwit (Coastal 4) and the Black-Tailed Godwit both have straight or upward curving bills; none of course have the distinguishing curlew call.

2. **Turnstone**

UNUSUAL AMONG WADERS IN preferring a rocky coast or pebble beach, the Turnstone is so called because it uses its stout, slightly upturned dark bill to flip over stones, seaweed and any other debris in search of invertebrate food. It feeds in small, closely packed groups who seem to bicker noisily amongst themselves as they scour the tide line for its rich pickings.

ARENARIA INTERPRES

Appearance: black, chestnut and white (tortoiseshell) mottled upper parts; white underparts; white neck and head, with bold black chest, neck and face markings and speckled black cap; short black bill and short orange legs. Flight reveals white back, rump and wing markings. In winter, back and head predominantly darker brown with black and white marbling.

Size: 23cm (9").

Voice: occasional staccato tut-tut; alarm is a fast low-pitched ti-ti-ti-ti-ti.

Habitat: rocky foreshores.

Distribution: August to May throughout Ireland and Britain except far north west of Scotland.

Not to be confused with: the Dunlin (Coastal 5), slightly smaller, with a darker back, plain buff breast, neck and head, black legs and a finer and slightly down-curving bill; and the Purple Sandpiper which shares the migration pattern of the Turnstone but has grey-brown and white speckling all over (fainter on an almost white belly), with only very faint chestnut on the wings, a longer bill and dull yellow legs.

Often seen in the company of the similar-shaped Purple Sandpiper, the Turnstone scavenges higher up the shore while its sandpiper companion prefers the water's edge. It is relatively unafraid of humans, and can also be seen on harbour walls.

It is absent from Britain in the summer months when it migrates to Scandinavian or Canadian shores in order to breed. In North America it is known more accurately as the Ruddy Turnstone, to differentiate it from the rarer Black Turnstone – only found migrating between Alaska and the American west coast.

3. Redshank

THE REDSHANK IS ONE OF THE most widespread of British shore birds, but is also not uncommon further inland, especially during breeding, where it can be just as at home on freshwater marshes as on the salt ones of the coast.

It has been found that allowing cattle to graze on the marshland breeding habitat of the Redshank (outwith the breeding period to avoid trampling the eggs) actually improves the environment for the bird, by reducing the height of growth and encouraging biodiversity of plant life. Redshank nests are more numerous on such grazed sites.

Redshank numbers have conversely suffered from the practise of draining wetlands to make them "useful", but it remains a common and colourful sight. The winter population is substantially increased by migrant birds from Iceland and elsewhere.

In estuaries as the tide rises it will crowd together with Dunlins, Oystercatchers and other species on the shrinking outcrops of higher ground. But otherwise it tends to keep itself separate from other birds, feeding in small groups with two or three other Redshanks.

TRINGA TOTANUS

Appearance: mottled dark brown upper parts and head; off-white speckled underparts; long bright orange-red legs (which trail behind tail in flight); dark eye with pale eye-ring; long straight red bill with black tip. In winter, belly is unmarked off-white, back is paler brown, and legs and bill lose some colouring. In flight white underwing, dark outer upper wing and broad white hindwing.

Size: 28cm (11").

Voice: tewk-ewk-ewk in alarm; song in flight to-you to-you to-you.

Habitat: salt and fresh water of all wetlands including uplands, but especially estuaries.

Distribution: all year throughout Britain and Ireland (less common in Southern Ireland).

Not to be confused with: the Greenshank, a slimmer, slightly larger bird of similar pattern but with an unmarked white belly, longer, slightly upturned grey-green bill and grey-green legs.

4. **Bar-Tailed Godwit**

IT IS THOUGHT THAT THE Godwit's strange name may be derived from the Anglo-Saxon expression mean-ing "good creature" – as in "good to eat"! It was much prized on the medieval dinner table, when a Godwit would fetch three times as much as a Snipe at market.

In Iceland the Godwit, in its Black-Tailed form, is called the Jardraeka, meaning "earth raker" – a reference to the habit in both species of feeding by searching deeply in the mud with its long bill for shellfish and worms.

The Bar-Tailed Godwit, like many waders, leaves Britain in the summer to breed on tundra in the far north of Scandinavia and Russia, where the male's chest and neck turn a fiery copper red for its courtship display.

LIMOSA LAPPONICA

Appearance: pale buff underparts, speckled at chest; salt-and-pepper grey-brown and buff upper parts (juvenile has more pronounced streaks); bold buff eyebrow; long thin pink bill, dark towards tip with very slight upwards curve; in flight, dark outer upper wing and distinctive dark-barred tail; male's breeding plumage (rarely seen in Britain) has rich orange-red underside.

Size: 38cm (15").

Voice: flight call of cowik-cowik-cowik.

Habitat: mudflats, estuaries and beaches.

Distribution: July to May throughout Britain and Ireland except western and northern Scotland.

Not to be confused with: the Black-Tailed Godwit, very similar but with longer legs and a distinguishing white bar along its wings in flight and of course a black tail without bars; the Curlew (Coastal 1) has colouring similar to the winter plumage of the Bar-Tailed Godwit, but its bill curves distinctly down, not up.

In recent years its cousin the Black-Tailed Godwit has started to breed in East Anglia and elsewhere, having been hunted to local extinction in the 19th century. It was known in the area as the Yarwhelp in reference to its loud call, a name preserved in local place-names such as Whelp Moor in Suffolk.

5. Dunlin

IN THE NORTH WEST OF IRELAND the Dunlin is a non-migratory resident, breeding and wintering in the same area. Elsewhere it is estimated that as many as 5000 pairs of Dunlin breed each summer in the secluded safety of Britain's remote moorland landscape, in northern England, Wales and Scotland, before migrating southwards to the coasts. But this is as nothing compared

to the more than 500,000 pairs who migrate to our island's coastline from Iceland and Scandinavia to feed through the winter months.

The Dunlin, whose name means literally "small and brown", is by far the commonest wader on Britain's shores, where it gathers along the water's edge in massive flocks to probe the beach with its inquisitive bill used like the needle on a sewing machine.

When they take to the air, flocks of Dunlin weave and dart as one with great co-ordination, flashing black and white as the birds show first their dark backs, then their pale bellies, with each mass change of direction.

CALIDRIS ALPINA

Appearance: white underparts; grey-brown head and back; indistinct grey-brown streaking on breast; pale buff eyebrow above dark eye; quite long tapering black bill with slight downward curve; short black legs. Flight reveals thin white wingbar, and dark brown rump with white sides. In summer, streaks on breast are dark brown and more sharply focused, back is mottled chestnut and black, and forebelly has large black patch.

Size: 18cm (7").

Voice: reedy spreep, extending in song to a longer "referee's whistle" blast.

Habitat: estuaries, flood plains, marshy fields.

Distribution: all year on British and Irish coasts, also inland further north during breeding season.

Not to be confused with: the Sanderling (Coastal 6) which has a shorter bill and in winter a grey-white head and greyer back; in summer the Sanderling has richer chestnut on back, head and chest, but not the distinctive black belly-patch of the Dunlin.

6. **Sanderling**

THE SANDERLING IS EASILY distinguishable as the palest of the British winter waders – in fact its Latin name means "the white wader". You will often get the chance for comparison

CALIDRIS ALBA

Appearance: pure white underparts; pale grey-brown upper parts with darker shoulders; white head with pale grey cap and eye stripe. Straight black bill and black legs; white wingbar and grey back revealed in flight. In summer head, back and chest turn rich tortoiseshell mix of chestnut, black and white.

Size: 20cm (8").

Voice: a sharp squeaky whit-whit.

Habitat: water's edge on sandy beaches, occasionally also rocky shores; breeds on Arctic tundra.

Distribution: July to May throughout England, Wales, Ireland and Southern Scotland.

Not to be confused with: the Knot, a bigger wader whose winter plumage is more grey all over (in summer it has pale orange under parts and head and a dark speckled chestnut back); the Dunlin (Coastal 5) is browner in winter and has the distinguishing black belly mark during summer breeding.

because they regularly associate with Dunlin, huddling together on shrinking patches of higher ground as the tide comes in.

The Sanderling can also be identified by its feeding habits. It likes the minute marine life which the tide delivers and which the breaking waves reveal. It will run in and out in groups of up to 50 as the waves come and go, snatching at worms, sandhoppers and small molluscs and crustaceans.

When disturbed by humans strolling along the beach, the Sanderling tends to run away ahead of them instead of flying off.

Like many waders, the Sanderling breeds far to the north on Arctic tundra, and occurs in Britain either as a winter visitor or, in autumn and spring, in transit to and from its other wintering grounds in Southern Europe and north Africa.

7. **Common Tern**

TERNS GENERALLY HAVE LONGER thinner bills than gulls (except of course for continental Europe's Gull-Billed Tern!) and gulls lack the typical black cap and forked tail of the tern family. Gulls are also more opportunistic scavengers in their feeding than terns.

STERNA HIRUNDO

Appearance: grey body above and below; darker outer feathers on wings; classic forked tern tail; white breast; white head with full black cap; bright orange-red bill with black tip; orange-red legs. Juveniles and winter adults have white forehead, darker bill and dark patch on shoulder; juveniles also have faint reddish brown barring on upper parts.

Size: 35cm (14").

Voice: fast insistent kiri-kiri-kiri, and a longer shrieked kre-yaar.

Habitat: sand and shingle on coasts and inland rivers, and increasingly on inland open freshwater.

Distribution: April to October throughout Ireland and Britain except south west Wales and inland south west England.

Not to be confused with: many other terns: the Arctic Tern has paler outer wings and no black tip to the bill in summer, and a slightly longer tail just visible beyond the folded wings; the Sandwich Tern (Coastal 20) is larger, with a spiky downward crest at the rear of its cap, black legs and a black bill with yellow tip; the rare Roseate Tern has paler grey upper parts and a hint of pink on its white underside.

Like all British terns the Common Tern hovers with a frantic flapping of its wings above the water to spot its prey before plunging below the surface in a stabbing dive, or swooping to grab fish or insects from the surface in flight.

Although different species of the tern family can be difficult to tell apart, the fact that they often congregate in each others' company means that you will often have ample opportunity to compare them and identify the subtle differences between them.

8. Ringed Plover

ALTHOUGH CLASSED AS A WADER, it might be more accurate to describe the Ringed Plover as a running bird – instead of sifting through water or mud for its food like most other species, the Plover races about and pounces on grubs and insects on the surface of the ground.

The Ringed Plover is one of those birds that pretend to be injured when their nest and brood are threatened by a predator, drawing the intruder to her and away from the vulnerable chicks. This subterfuge may have given rise to the old saying, "It's a long way from home that the Plover cries."

CHARADRIUS HIATICULA

Appearance: grey brown upper parts with dark tail tip; white underparts; broad black band around neck and breast and bold black eye-mask; white eyebrow and grey-brown cap; short orange bill with black tip; orange legs; white wingbar visible in flight. The black neck band fades to grey-brown on the winter adult, and is incomplete at the front of the juvenile bird. The bill is much duller on both the juvenile and the winter adult.

Size: 18cm (7").

Voice: a mellow high-pitched whistled to-wee, becoming a sharper twee when alarmed; in spring this is developed with churrs and clicks into a display trill.

Habitat: shores and estuaries of mud, sand or shingle; less common inland.

Distribution: all year throughout Britain and Ireland.

Not to be confused with: the Little Ringed Plover, only slightly smaller with an all-black bill, no white wingbar, dull pink legs, a narrower breast band and a bright yellow eye-ring; the Kentish Plover, now alas extremely rare even in Kent and absent from the rest of Britain (though still quite common on the shores of mainland Europe), has dark legs and bill, incomplete breast band and slightly richer brown upper parts, especially a ginger cap in summer.

9. Grey Plover

LIKE MANY WADERS, THE GREY Plover will not fly away as the rising tide covers its habitat, but merely pulls into ever closer-packed flocks as the waters advance around it. At this stage it will cluster together with other breeds of wader, unlike its close cousin the Golden Plover (which tends not to mix).

The English name for this family of birds derives from the French version, pluvier, meaning "rain bird". In the same vein, the German name (Regenpfeiffer) means "rain whistler", and traditionally the autumn arrival of the birds in British estuaries from their Arctic breeding grounds heralded the return of rain after summer.

In Ireland there was a tradition that a Grey Plover standing silently in a field would forecast a frosty night – but since the birds are principally winter migrants there, this was perhaps a shrewd and safe Irish bet!

PLUVIALIS SQUATAROLA

Appearance: mottled grey-brown upper parts; off-white underside; square-set black bill with a stubby tip; darker areas on head at cap and around eye; in flight, white wingbar on upper wing, black armpit on lower, white tail and rump, with dark brown bars on tail; dark grey legs. In summer the upper parts are a bolder mottle of black, grey and white; the under parts turn black from the eye to before the tail, with a wide band of white above that from forehead to side.

Size: 28cm (11").

Voice: a falling-then-rising whistle, slaw-wee.

Habitat: estuaries and mudflats; very rare inland.

Distribution: Autumn to April throughout Britain and Ireland, rarer in west.

Not to be confused with: the more widespread Golden Plover, in all seasons similar in pattern (except the grey's distinctive black armpit) but with a shorter bill, and replacing the silver-grey markings with golden buff-yellow; in winter, the Knot, a smaller wader, is similar but with greyer upper parts and a longer bill.

10. Brent Goose

THE PALE-BELLIED AND DARK-bellied versions of the Brent Goose are considered two races of the same species, and they live quite separate migratory lives. The dark-bellied Brent breeds in Siberia and winters in south east England (and on the other side of the Channel from Denmark to Brittany). The pale-bellied bird that migrates to Ireland and north eastern England travels from Greenland.

The Brent Goose has begun to develop a taste for farm-grown cereals and can increasingly be seen in fields of such crops beside the sea. But it remains extremely dependent on the foods of its natural estuary habitat – algae, and eelgrass. A disastrous disease which almost wiped out eelgrass in Europe in the 1930s also reduced the

BRANTA BERNICLA

Appearance: dark grey-brown upper parts; underparts white at rear and either warm mid-brown or dirty brown off-white from legs forward; chest, neck and head all black, with small white blotch below head on side of neck; short black bill; sturdy black legs. Juveniles lack the white neck patch.

Size: 60cm (24").

Voice: coarse, throaty cronk-cronk.

Habitat: large muddy estuaries.

Distribution: September to April throughout Ireland and in east and south of England.

Not to be confused with: the Canada Goose, a much larger goose with a pale buff breast below its black neck and head, and a white patch slung from ear to ear under its chin; and the Barnacle Goose, which has a mid-grey back with black bars, a very pale grey belly, and a white face with a black stripe between the eyes.

Brent Goose population to a quarter of its size. Happily both grass and bird have since recovered.

The Arctic breeding cycle of the Brent Goose is extremely vulnerable to climate, which normally allows them the briefest of windows in the harsh Arctic weather, between late June and August. A late spring may delay nesting, or allow predators to cross the ice to reach breeding islands; a wet spring may flood the nest sites.

11. Shag

LIKE THE CORMORANT, THE SHAG has a distinctive habit of perching, wings half-open on a rock, either for preening and display, or to dry itself, or perhaps to ease digestion after a large meal.

The Shag and the Cormorant are close relatives in the same ornithological family – the Shag is sometimes known as the Green Cormorant – and can be very hard to tell apart, especially at a distance. But there are tell-tale signs of habit and habitat.

For example, both dive from the water's surface, not from flight, to catch fish. But the Cormorant can undertake longer dives than the Shag, and the Shag sits slightly higher in the water than the Cormorant when swimming. The Shag is more confined in its habitat, restricting itself to remote and dangerous rocky waters and tides – it rarely strays inland or near human features such as harbours.

References to the Shag have been found in written records as early as the 8th century. And its remains have been found on British archaeological sites dating from as early as the late Stone Age, when man was still a hunter-gatherer and not yet a herder-farmer.

PHALACROCORAX ARISTOTELIS

Appearance: tall, all-black body with iridescent green; quite long black neck and head, with steep forehead and green eye; long, shallow black and yellow bill with slight hook at end; during breeding, tufted display crest on forehead. Winter adults and juveniles may have white markings on chin. Juvenile has dark brown upper parts, slightly paler below.

Size: 75cm (30").

Voice: a rattling chatter of grunts and clicks.

Habitat: cliffs on rocky coasts and islands.

Distribution: all year in Ireland and northern and western coasts of Britain; rare in south east and inland.

Not to be confused with: the Cormorant (Coastal 12), a larger heavier-built bird with slower wingbeat than the Shag; the Cormorant has a white chin, shallower forehead, deeper bill with more yellow at base and more pronounced hook at tip.

12. **Cormorant**

THE CORMORANT'S NAME MEANS "raven of the sea", a reference not only to its colour but to its coarse croaking. It is sometimes known as the Great Cormorant to distinguish it from the smaller Green Cormorant (the less common name for the Shag). The first Cormorants appeared on the world's seas 100 million years ago.

PHALACROCORAX CARBO

Appearance: tall, all-black body with a grey-green lustre on the back; white patch on thigh disappears after breeding; long black neck and large head with white face below eyes; bare orange-yellow skin at bill, which is long and stout with distinct small hook at the tip.

Size: 90cm (36").

Voice: a guttural cackle, a croaky crooning in display.

Habitat: sheltered bays and estuaries including harbours; also on fresh water further inland, especially in winter.

Distribution: all year near western and northern coasts of Britain and Ireland, and further inland in southern England; less common in east, except in winter.

Not to be confused with: the Shag (Coastal 11), significantly smaller and without any white markings on face or thigh; the Shag also has quicker wingbeats in flight and flies across the surface of the water, much lower than the Cormorant.

The similarity between the Cormorant and its cousin the Shag causes much confusion. But there are several ways of separating them. For example, although both birds swim with head tilted upwards, the Cormorant sits lower in the water; sometimes its back seems completely submerged.

The Cormorant tolerates a wider range of habitats than the Shag, including gentler, more sheltered shores and man-made environments such as marinas and harbour waters. It is correspondingly a commoner sight than the smaller bird. Where the Shag confines itself to cliffs and caves, the Cormorant is as likely to build its nest in a tree as on a ledge.

It is the Cormorant which Japanese and Chinese fishermen have trained to dive for fish for over 1300 years, fitting a ring around their necks to prevent them from swallowing their catch.

13. Oyster-catcher

OYSTERCATCHERS GATHER IN their thousands in their winter coastal feeding grounds, where the sheer volume of their massed choir is a spectacular British wildlife experience.

They feed on the molluscs and worms they root out from mudflats, seaweed and rocky shores. The relatively stout bill is specially adapted for breaking open the shells, and Oystercatchers are sometimes considered a pest by commercial shell-fisheries. A large cull of the birds was ordered in the 1970s, from which they have since recovered.

Oystercatchers actually prefer mussels to oysters. Each bird has its own technique for cracking open the shells, which it learns from its parent birds.

In the breeding season they congregate in smaller numbers in the north,

HAEMATOPUS OSTRALEGUS

Appearance: striking black upper parts and white lower, with short dark tail; matt black head with bright red eye and quite long bold orange bill; grey-pink legs; flight shows white rump and bold white wingbar. In winter a white neck ring, and black tip to bill. Juvenile similar to adult winter plumage, with dark brown upper parts.

Size: 42cm (17").

Voice: a piercing kip-kip-kip, growing into a shrill chorus of keep-keep-keep from a large flock.

Habitat: beaches of all sorts, also in the north breeding further inland on river shores and riverside fields.

Distribution: all year throughout Britain and Ireland.

Not to be confused with: the Black-Tailed Godwit which is similar in flight, but has greyer inner wings, a much longer bill and longer legs which trail behind the tail.

often far inland along streams and even on moorsides, where they root about for food in much the same way they would on their coastal preserves.

The Oystercatcher is considered by ornithologists to be one of the relatively few genuinely cosmopolitan birds – ones which occur all over the world as the same species rather than relatives within the same family. Other British birds falling into this category include the Moorhen and the Barn Owl.

14. Great Black-Backed Gull

THE GREAT BLACK-BACKED GULL is the largest gull in the world, and quite easy to identify amongst the others because of its pure black back and wings. Although not as numerous as those other large British gulls, the Lesser Black-Backed Gull and the Herring Gull, it is dominant wherever it appears, and has significantly expanded its population in recent years.

Both the Great and the Lesser Black-Backed Gull are fiercely aggressive, so predatory of some smaller seabirds such as Manx Sheerwater and Puffin that they are now considered a significant threat to

those species on which they prey.

Although the black back of the adult makes the Great Black-Backed Gull unmistakable, immature gulls can be difficult to identify when they all seem to be a scruffy blotchy brown. But even as a juvenile, the Great Black-Backed Gull has a larger, stouter bill than other large gulls.

It also has the most sharply defined patterns of brown and white on its back and generally less speckling on its breast and neck than young Herring Gulls or Lesser Black-Backed Gulls. Herring Gull young are the palest brown of the three.

LARUS MARINUS

Appearance: very large gull, with black back and wings; white under parts, neck and head; stout yellow bill with large red spot near tip on lower jaw; pale-grey-pink legs; faint grey-brown shading on cap in winter. In flight, white tail, and large white tip and white trailing edge to wing; Juveniles have mottled dark brown and white back and wings and black bill.

Size: 70cm (28").

Voice: deep rasping crawk, which can be a repetitive rattle in alarm, and developed into a squealing laugh in display.

Habitat: rocky coasts; in winter other beaches and human habitation such as rubbish tips and reservoirs.

Distribution: all year throughout coastal Britain and Ireland, in winter also further inland.

Not to be confused with: the Lesser Black-Backed Gull (Coastal 15), which has yellow legs, and can have quite a dark grey but never black back.

15. Lesser Black-Backed Gull

IDENTIFYING GULLS CAN BE A daunting task for the inexperienced birdwatcher. A good quick guide to the three large gulls of Britain is: black back and pink legs – Great Black-Backed Gull; both bill and legs yellow – Lesser Black-Backed Gull; pale grey back and pink legs – Herring Gull. The Lesser Black-Backed Gull also has a noticeably smaller bill than the others.

There are several sub-species of the Lesser Black-Backed Gull which account for the various shades of grey in which it can be seen. A version from north western Europe is the palest, one from Holland is a little darker than the British edition, and a Scandinavian variety is the darkest of all. But none achieve the true black of the Great Black-Backed Gull.

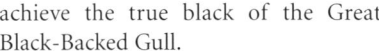

LARUS FUSCUS

Appearance: large gull with dark grey (or, less commonly, paler grey) back and wings; white under parts, neck and head; bill yellow with red spot near tip on lower jaw; bright yellow tail, black wing tips with white dot, dark grey band to rear of underwing. In winter bill is blackened, legs are greyer and there is marked grey-brown shading to head and neck. Juveniles have dappled grey-brown and white back, breast and head, and black bill.

Size: 60cm (24").

Voice: throaty, repeated key-ow-ow-ow; thin, rough, laughing gya-gya-gya in display.

Habitat: summer on cliffs, islands and open moorlands; winter on beaches, farmland, reservoirs and rubbish tips.

Distribution: all year throughout Britain and Ireland; less common in the north in winter.

Not to be confused with: the Great Black-Backed Gull (Coastal 14), which is larger, genuinely black, with pink not yellow legs and bolder white patches on its wingtips; the Herring Gull (Coastal 16), which has pink legs and more white spots on its wingtips; the Yellow-Legged Gull is very similar, but a rare passing visitor to the south of England – it has a slightly paler grey back and more pronounced black and white wingtips.

16. Herring Gull

LARUS ARGENTATUS

Appearance: large gull with pale grey back and wings; white under parts, neck and head; pale eye, and yellow bill with red spot near tip on lower jaw; pale pink legs. In flight, white tail, black wingtips with white spots, and pale grey band to rear of under-wing; in winter, grey-brown streaking on head. Juveniles have blotchy brown body and head, and black bill.

Size: 60cm (24").

Voice: squealing, squeaky kee-yow-ow-ow; powerful, loud, laughing ha-ya-ya-ya in display.

Habitat: summer on cliffs and islands; winter on beaches, farmland, reservoirs and rubbish tips.

Distribution: all year throughout Ireland and Britain; less common in south west England.

Not to be confused with: the Lesser Black-Backed Gull (Coastal 15), generally a darker grey and with yellow not pink legs; the Yellow-Legged Gull, very similar except in the colour of its legs; the Common Gull, similar at a glance but much smaller, with a dark eye, slim all-yellow bill and greeny yellow legs; the Kittiwake (Coastal 22), also superficially similar, is smaller still, with a dark eye, no white on black wingtips and distinguishing short black legs.

THE HERRING GULL IS THE commonest of the large British gulls, a frequent sight both on the coast (where in towns it may even be considered a pest) and just about anywhere inland as well.

The Herring Gull takes three years to reach maturity. Its piercing and incessant shrieking is a familiar sound of the harbourside – higher-pitched than the throaty Lesser Black-Backed Gull, while the rasping Great Black-Backed Gull's voice is deeper still.

Although not as aggressive as either of the Black-Backed Gulls, the Herring Gull substantially increased in numbers during the 20th century, and was the subject of conservation controls to prevent it from becoming too prevalent at the expense of other, rarer birds. In the last 25 years however it has gone into a slight and unexplained decline, and now more than half the 165,000 breeding pairs nest in less than ten locations.

17. **Fulmar**

ALTHOUGH IT RESEMBLES A GULL, the Fulmar belongs to the petrel family. The name means "foul gull" in Icelandic, a reference to its well-known defence tactic of spitting a foul-smelling oil with great accuracy at any intruder to its nest – something to which cliff-climbers and bird-ringers will ruefully testify!

Fulmars are effortless flyers, skimming the ocean surface with barely a wingbeat, or soaring up cliff faces to their nesting ledges. Their young are reported to spend the first four years of their lives entirely at sea, and a further three years perching at nesting sites before they actually start to breed, laying only one egg a year. They can live for 30 or 40 years.

The longevity of the Fulmar has contributed to the astonishing spread of its range over the last 200 years, as young adult birds have been forced to look further and further for vacant nesting sites. Starting in the early 19th century from just two of its nesting grounds – remote St Kilda west of Scotland and the westman islands off Iceland – Fulmars have colonised the entire coastline of the British Isles. Only the present decline in the fishing industry, whose fleets the Fulmar follows for scraps, has had any restraining effect on its seemingly relentless population explosion.

FULMARUS GLACIALIS

Appearance: gull-like bird with light grey back and wings, with darker grey wingtips and paler tail; white under parts, short white neck and rounded white head; yellow and grey hooked bill, with distinctive petrel nostril tube on top jaw; pale red legs and webbed feet. Flight reveals a pale patch just before the wingtips.

Size: 48cm (19").

Voice: a harsh cackle during breeding, which gives way to a droning murmured chuckle.

Habitat: breeds on ledges of cliffs and, rarely, buildings; also on turf on islands; spends the rest of its life at sea.

Distribution: all year throughout coastal Britain and Ireland.

Not to be confused with: the Herring Gull (Coastal 16) and the Iceland Gull, both slightly larger and paler grey, with the gull's characteristic red dot on the bill and without the Fulmar's characteristic nostril tube.

18. **Razorbill**

THE RAZORBILL IS OF THE AUK family, the closest living relative of the now-extinct Great Auk, which was

ALCA TORDA

Appearance: thick-set seabird. White underparts; black back, wings, solid neck and large rounded head; pointed black tail and rump with white sides; horizontal white stripe running forward from eye; large thick hooked black bill with a white vertical band around it near the tip; short white-feathered legs above black feet. In winter the eye stripe disappears and the neck turns off-white.

Size: 40cm (16").

Voice: a long growling urrr in colonies; silent at sea.

Habitat: breeds on rocky coasts of cliff and boulder; otherwise at sea, including estuaries and bays.

Distribution: all year throughout Britain and Ireland except south east England, more common on western and northern coasts.

Not to be confused with: other auks, particularly the slightly larger Guillemot (Coastal 21) which shares the Razorbill's penguin-like stance and markings but has a much finer, dagger-like bill and, in flight, a more square-cut, less pointed tail.

hunted out of existence in the 19th century for food and feathers. Ironically its end was hastened by ornithologists who, aware of its dwindling numbers, raced to collect its rare eggs.

The Great Auk was easily trapped, being a flightless bird with tiny, useless wings. Although the Razorbill can fly strongly, it shares the short-wing characteristic of all auks, giving it a flight of rapid, whirring wingbeats.

The Razorbill's legs, set far back on its body, force it to stand upright like a Penguin. On land it is an ungainly, waddling walker. But like the Penguin, the Razorbill folds its legs conveniently away in the water, when it dives constantly and purposefully from the surface to great depths in search of fish, using its fin-like wings to propel it below the surface. Like all diving seabirds, the Razorbill is vulnerable to pollution at sea, and to declining fish stocks.

19. **Puffin**

THE PUFFIN SHARES THE FEATURES of all auks, specially adapted for diving

for its food – legs set well back on the body and short wings, all making for an easier passage through the water. On land the auk waddle and extraordinary multi-coloured bill have often led to descriptions of the Puffin as the clown of the seabird kingdom, and to its nick-name the sea parrot.

It still nests in large colonies, typically burrowing into the turf on remote islands and shorelines, or borrowing old rabbit warrens for the purpose. Unfortunately the very act of tunnelling its nests is eroding this habitat, and Puffins are adapting to other holes such as cavities in cliffs and boulders for use as nests.

Like all auks the diving Puffin is very vulnerable to water pollution and a frequent victim of oil spillages at sea. The Puffin population is in decline at present.

FRATERCULA ARCTICA

Appearance: small round seabird. White underparts; black upper parts, tail, wings, neck and head; large white cheek, with distinctive dark eye and laughter-line crease running back from it; tall triangular bill dusky blue near face, orange-red at tip, with dividing vertical yellow lines; bright yellow-orange legs; in winter cheeks are greyer and bill loses layers and much of its colour. Juvenile resembles winter adult with smaller darker bill.

Size: 30cm (12").

Voice: a gentle coo-ing groan coo-aah.

Habitat: breeds in holes in cliffs, and tunnels in grass or scree slopes on islands and mainland coasts; otherwise far out to sea.

Distribution: March to November in Britain and Ireland but not on southern and eastern coasts of England and Ireland.

Not to be confused with: the Little Auk, a much smaller bird with an all black head in summer (white below and behind eye in winter) and only a stubby, almost finch-like black bill.

20. Sandwich Tern

THE SANDWICH TERN BREEDS IN Britain in huge, noisy, densely packed colonies on sand dunes and other soft shores, before migrating to Africa for the winter. Although birds may return to the same ternery for several seasons, they are also likely to abandon a site suddenly for reasons not clear, at least to human beings.

Terns used to be known as sea-swallows because of their forked tails. In flight the Sandwich Tern's wings are so pale as to be almost white, with only the dark extremities of wingtips, head and feet standing out. When feeding, it hovers on fast wingbeats before diving with a loud splash to collect sand eels or other fish from the sea.

In the 19th century the Sandwich Tern had been hunted nearly to extinction on the south coast of England – including ironically the area around the town of Sandwich in Kent from which it gets its name. Happily it has recovered, and now occurs all over the world, making it what ornithologists call a cosmopolitan bird – one which is seen everywhere as the same species, not just as different members of the same bird family.

STERNA SANDVICENSIS

Appearance: gull-like bird. Very pale grey upper parts; white underparts, breast and lower face; black cap including eye and running back to spiky black downward crest on back of neck; long fine black bill with yellow tip; black legs; in flight, forked white tail, grey wings with darker bars at tips. After nesting, cap shrinks to back of head, replaced by all-white neck and forehead.

Size: 40cm (16").

Voice: a balanced but harsh kirr-rick repeated; sometimes a faster and rising ki-rick.

Habitat: sand dunes, sand and shingle beaches.

Distribution: March to October throughout coastal Britain and Ireland.

Not to be confused with: the Common Tern (Coastal 7), a slightly smaller bird with no crest, and an orange bill and legs; the Roseate Tern has a bold black streak at the wingtips, a red base to its black bill and red legs.

21. **Guillemot**

THE GUILLEMOT OCCURS IN TWO forms – those in the north are almost black in colour, while those further south are distinctly brown (and correspondingly easier to tell apart from Razorbills). A further variation exists in the Bridled Guillemot, so-called because of its white eye-ring and a white line running backwards from it like a rein.

Guillemots are magnificent divers, reaching depths of up to 50m. They winter far out at sea, but during breeding can often be seen floating in large groups on the inshore waters beneath their cliff nesting sites. They don't in fact build nests, and on a bare ledge they lay one egg a year. The egg has evolved to be pear-shaped rather than oval or round, to prevent it from rolling away over the edge.

The Protection of Birds Act of 1954 outlawed the last surviving "harvest" of Guillemot eggs, which used to take place annually in May at Bempton Cliffs near Flamborough Head. Up to 400 hundred eggs a day were taken during the season by men lowered precariously down the cliff-face in search of a boost to their incomes. These days, Bempton Cliffs is an important RSPB Bird Sanctuary.

URIA AALGE

Appearance: stout seabird. White underparts; black or very dark brown tail, back, wings, and relatively slim neck and head; dark eye and long thin sharp black bill; short white-feathered legs and black feet; flight reveals short square tail, and thin white trailing edge on wing. Juveniles and winter adults have white cheek and throat, with black line running back from eye.

Size: 43cm (17").

Voice: a long, growling aa-rrr, or shorter repetitive arr-arr-arr.

Habitat: ledges and tops of cliffs during breeding; otherwise inshore or further out to sea.

Distribution: all year throughout Britain and Ireland; less common in south-east England.

Not to be confused with: the Razorbill (Coastal 18), a slightly smaller auk of stockier build, with a much thicker bill marked with horizontal and vertical white lines.

22. **Kittiwake**

THE GERMAN, FRENCH AND LATIN terms for this bird mean "three-toed gull", because its hind toe is either very small or absent altogether. But in most other languages where the Kittiwake occurs, it is named after its distinctive piercing chorus. In Greenland it is the tatavaq, in Orkney the kishiefaik, in Finland the pikkukajava, and in Newfoundland the tickle-arse! Juvenile Kittiwakes were known as Tarrocks by fishermen.

Kittiwakes are extremely noisy birds, breeding in very large colonies, their nests perched on the smallest ledges. They often share their breeding grounds with members of the auk family – Puffins, Razorbills and Guillemots.

Kittiwakes are among the first birds on written record in modern times, in a 7th century poem called "The Seafarer". The poet, clearly a keen bird-watcher, describes accurately half a dozen species including the Kitti-wake which he observes one day in April on the Bass Rock in the Firth of Forth, near present-day Edinburgh.

LARUS TRIDACTYLA

Appearance: medium gull. Mid-grey back and wings with black wingtips; white tail, under parts, neck and rounded head; dark eye; quite short all-yellow bill; short black legs. Juvenile has distinctive bold black W across wingspan, black bar at end of tail and black half-collar behind neck. Winter adult has grey markings on head.

Size: 40cm (16").

Voice: a ringing and repeated kitt-i-wa-a-ake.

Habitat: breeds on narrow cliff ledges, winters at sea.

Distribution: all year throughout Ireland and Britain, especially on northern and western coasts; less common inshore in winter.

Not to be confused with: the Common Gull, which has yellow-green legs and a bold white spot on its black wingtips; the Herring Gull (Coastal 16) is much bigger, with pink legs, white spots on the black wingtips and a red spot under the tip of its bill; the juvenile Little Gull has a similar but browner W on its wing – it is more common as a winter visitor.

23. **Gannet**

GANNETS FEED BY DIVING FROM great heights – up to 30 metres, 100 feet – onto mackerel and other fish. When they spot a shoal, the birds will gather in animated clouds above it, wheeling and plunging in a thrilling spectacle.

They nest in large colonies on long-established sites, some well over a thousand years old. Nests are so closely packed that birds could touch each other. Pairs perform courtship dances which include mock-duelling with their bills.

Gannets have been a prey for man since the early Stone Age. Harvesting of eggs and chicks of seabirds still goes on in the Faeroe Isles and in Iceland, and persisted in this country until being made illegal in 1954.

To this day one hunting expedition is exempt from the ban. In a tradition dating back to at least 1549, 10 men from Lewis sail to the Gannet colony on Sula Sgeir and cull about 2000 gugas (as the young birds are known), salting them on the island before returning to sell them as a delicacy.

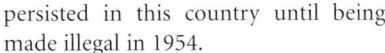

SULA BASSANA

Appearance: large seabird. White body, neck and head with very pale orange shading on back of head; large, dagger-shaped bill with dark horizontal grooves; bare black legs and feet. In flight, bold black wingtips and narrow, pointed white tail. Juvenile is a mottled dark brown all over, with white V above tail, body becoming piebald then white with maturity.

Size: 90cm (36").

Voice: a honking, hoarse urr-urr-urr, varying in pitch and rhythm.

Habitat: colonies on cliffs and steep slopes; otherwise some distance out to sea.

Distribution: March to October at colonies throughout Britain and southern Ireland.

Not to be confused with: the immature Great Black-Backed Gull (Coastal 14) may be mistaken for the darkly mottled young gannet.

24. **Rock Pipit**

THE ROCK PIPIT DARTS BACK AND forth, with a walk not a hop, feeding on insects it finds amongst the grass, sand and stones of Britain's shoreline. In summer it prefers the more remote locations of cliff and island, nesting in tiny cavities in the rocks. In winter it moves to the more open and gentle habitats of beach and mudflat.

Pipits can be extremely difficult to tell apart, with often just the very subtlest of variations of streaky brown! Indeed ornithologists themselves only began to recognise them as separate species in the course of the 18th century.

It helps that they very rarely share a habitat. The Tree Pipit lives on the edge of woodland (in summer only), the Rock Pipit on the edge of the sea. The Meadow Pipit spends the summer on moorland and the winter on lowland, the Water Pipit visits only the south of England and only in winter, at a variety of fresh- and saltwater habitats, unlike the strictly coastal Rock Pipit. Happily for British birdwatchers, these are the only four from a total of 39 Pipit species occurring globally to visit our islands!

ANTHUS PETROSUS

Appearance: small brown bird. Streaky olive-brown upper parts; underparts grey-buff with bold dark brown streaks; buff throat and eyebrow; dark eye in thin pale eye-ring; quite long black bill; upper leg buff-feathered, lower bare black-brown; in flight, dark brown tail with grey sides.

Size: 16cm (6").

Voice: a strong, rounded, reedy single seep, developed by repetition into song with a rasping metallic trill at the end.

Habitat: rocky shores, and softer coastal areas in winter.

Distribution: all year throughout Britain and Ireland except less rocky eastern coasts.

Not to be confused with: the Meadow Pipit (Country 9) which has reddish legs, a similar but weaker voice, and white sides to its tail instead of grey.

Appendix A: Quick Reference

At-a-glance differences between some commonly confused birds.

Big Black Birds

RAVEN (63cm)
All black, diamond tail, fingered wingtips.

CARRION CROW (Country 4) (47cm)
All black, grey legs, square tail, square wings – England, Wales, SE Scotland.

HOODED CROW (Country 4) (47cm)
Grey body, grey legs, square tail – Isle of Man, NW England, Scotland, Ireland.

ROOK (Country 1) (45cm)
All black, bare white skin at base of bill, rounded tail, wings more pointed than Carrion Crow.

CHOUGH (39cm)
More slender down-curved red bill, red legs, square tail, square fingered wingtips – west coasts only, rare.

JACKDAW (Country 5) (34cm)
Grey on sides and back of head, pale grey eyes – much smaller bird.

Little Brown Birds

The commonest little brown bird is the House Sparrow. The descriptions below its entry are comparisons to it.

HOUSE SPARROW (Urban 16) (14cm)
Thickset black bill, white flash on wings (male only), black throat, grey cheeks, plain grey breast, grey cap, dark tail.

MEADOW PIPIT (Country 9) (14cm)
Fine dark bill, cream stripe above eye and below cheek, dark spots on cream breast, white sides to tail.

TREE SPARROW (14cm)
Thickset black bill, black throat, black spot on white cheeks, grey-buff breast, chestnut brown cap.

DUNNOCK (Urban 17) (14cm)
Fine dark bill, grey throat, brown cheeks, plain grey-brown breast.

LINNET (FEMALE) (Country 20) (13cm)
Thickset grey bill, grey head, pale spot on grey cheek, buff breast.

ROBIN (JUVENILE) (Urban 8) (12cm)
Short fine dark bill, speckled brown and red body.

WREN (Urban 9) (9cm)
Fine dark bill, cream stripe above eye, buff breast – much smaller bird.

Seagulls

All gulls' heads acquire a grey-brown speckle in winter. Except as noted, all have yellow bills, white heads and white dots on black wingtips. Otherwise, in order of size:

GREAT BLACK-BACKED GULL (Coastal 14) (70cm)
Pink legs, black back, pale eye – largest bird.

LESSER BLACK-BACKED GULL (Coastal 15) (60cm)
Yellow legs, mid-grey back, pale eye, smaller bill.

HERRING GULL (Coastal 16) (60cm)
Pink legs, pale grey back, pale eye.

COMMON GULL (41cm)
Yellow legs, mid-grey back, dark eye.

KITTIWAKE (Coastal 22) (40cm)
Short dark legs, mid-grey back, dark eye, no white dot on wingtips.

BLACK-HEADED GULL (Urban 6) (36cm)
Orange-red legs and bill, very pale grey back, chocolate brown face and forehead (summer only), dark eye with white eyeing, large white front edge on upper wing.

LITTLE GULL (26cm)
Red legs, pale grey back, black bill, black head (summer only), no black wingtips.

TERNS can be distinguished from gulls by their black caps and forked swallow-like tails. Unlike gulls, terns feed on the wing.

Appendix B

Further Information

1. The Bird-Watching Code

A number of organisations, magazines and websites concerned with the watching and welfare of wild birds have agreed a common Code of Conduct for birdwatchers. It boils down to five simple "rules":

Avoid disturbing birds and their habitats – the interest of the birds always comes first. Talk quietly. Watch where you're putting your feet. Don't bring a dog. Don't wear bright colours. Don't confuse birds with recorded birdsong.

Be an ambassador for birdwatching. Share your enthusiasm with others. Encourage them to follow the Birdwatching Code. Use local services – benefits to them may also help preserve the birds' habitat.

Know the law and the rules for visiting the countryside, and follow them. Respect the wishes of local residents and landowners. Never take eggs. It is illegal to disturb or damage the sites of protected birds and other sites of scientific interest.

Send your sightings to the County Bird Recorder and to www.birdtrack.net. Your records are important for monitoring bird populations and movements, and for supporting local conservation.

Think about the interests of wildlife and local people before passing on news of a rare bird, especially during the breeding season. Too much human attention could drive the bird away or destroy its habitat.

2. Bird Organisations

Local clubs

Your local library will have information about your local birdwatching club. In addition, many websites carry national listings of bird clubs and societies, including:

http://www.birding.uk.com/links/Clubs-Societies.html
http://www.birdsofbritain.co.uk/bird-clubs/index.htm

Association of County Recorders and Editors

A list of local county recorders can be found at
http://www.britishbirds.co.uk/countyrecorders.htm
ACRE was formed in 1993 to establish common recording criteria in order to attain some national uniformity in the recording of bird reports.

British Trust for Ornithology

The Nunnery, Thetford, Norfolk, IP24 2PU
01842 750050
http://www.bto.org
The BTO promotes bird conservation through volunteer-based surveys. It also has offices in Scotland, Wales and Northern Ireland.

Royal Society for the Protection of Birds

The Lodge, Sandy, Bedfordshire, SG19 2DL
01767 680551
http://www.rspb.org.uk
The RSPB works to secure a healthy environment for birds and wildlife. It has 13 regional offices and over 150 reserves throughout the United Kingdom.

Wildfowl and Wetlands Trust
Slimbridge, Gloucestershire, GL2 7BT
01453 891900
http://www.wwt.org.uk
The WWT's mission is to conserve wetlands and their biodiversity. It has nine
visitor centres throughout the United Kingdom.

3. **Bird Reserves**

To give you some idea of the abundant opportunities for watching birds that exist in Britain and Ireland, the eight websites below carry between them information about at least 2139 different nature reserves wholly or partly dedicated to birdlife.

The RSPB has over 150 Bird Reserves throughout the United Kingdom:
http://www.rspb.org.uk/reserves/

The Wildfowl and Wetlands Trust has nine visitor centres throughout the United Kingdom:
http://www.wwt.org.uk/visit/

British Wildlife Trusts manage over 500 Wildlife Reserves:
http://www.wildlifetrusts.org/index.php?section=places:reserves

English Nature manages 215 National Nature Reserves and 1050 Local Nature Reserves:
http://www.english-nature.org.uk/

The Countryside Council for Wales website has 24 National Nature Reserves:
http://www.ccw.gov.uk/places/index.cfm?Action=Reserves&lang=en

Scottish Natural Heritage manages 66 National Nature Reserves and many more Local Nature Reserves:
http://www.nnr-scotland.org.uk/

In Northern Ireland the Environment and Heritage Service manages 47 Nature Reserves and one Marine Nature Reserve:
http://www.ehsni.gov.uk/natural/designated/nature_reserves.shtml

In the Republic of Ireland the National Parks and Wildlife Service manages 77 Nature Reserves:
http://www.npws.ie/NatureReserves/

The pictures in this book were provided courtesy of the following:

PAPILIO
Tel: +44 (0)1227 360996
www.papiliophotos.com

RICHARD FORD
www.digitalwildlife.co.uk

CORBIS
www.corbis.com

GETTY IMAGES
www.gettyimages.com

Design and artwork by Jane Stephens

Image research by Ellie Charleston

Published by Green Umbrella Publishing

Publishers Jules Gammond and Vanessa Gardner

Written by Colin Salter